The

Bravest

Thing

Donna Jo Napoli

MIDDLE SCHOOL IMC
CAMBRIDGE, WI

SCHOLASTIC INC.
New York Toronto London Auckland Sydney
Mexico City New Delhi Hong Kong Buenos Aires

ISBN 0-439-36798-0

Copyright © 1995 by Donna Jo Napoli. All rights reserved. Published by Scholastic Inc., 557 Broadway, New York, NY 10012, by arrangement with Puffin Books, a member of Penguin Putnam Inc. SCHOLASTIC and associated logos are trademarks and/or registered trademarks of Scholastic Inc.

12 11 10 9 8 7 6 5 4 3 2   3 4 5 6 7 8/0

Printed in the U.S.A.   40

First Scholastic printing, March 2003

With love for Eva,
who knows what a rabbit knows

—Mamma

Contents

➥ The Bravest Thing

1

Death

It all started with a death.

Two, actually.

We were coming home from Aunt Lizzy's house. She lives in Charleston, South Carolina, which is a giant tourist trap, my father says, but beautiful, my mother says. (My mother is Aunt Lizzy's sister.)

We stopped for dinner, and Mom let Arthur and me go into the shop next door to the restaurant. (Arthur is my little brother. He's six.) Arthur found a corncob pipe in the bathroom. I promised not to tell Mom where he found it because if she found out, she'd make him throw it away. And I told him he owed me big.

I looked around the shop for something nice to

give to Rodriguez. Like dried brine shrimp. Rodriguez used to gobble up those smelly little things fast. But they had nothing like that at the shop, even though Charleston is pretty close to the sea. Instead, I bought licorice and went to the car to put a small bite into Rodriguez's fishbowl. He had his own big tank with a rock at home, but he travels in a little fishbowl—or did, I mean. That's when I found him dead.

Mom helped me bury him in the dirt near the parking lot. She said, "Rodriguez had a good long life for a newt."

I blinked back my tears. "Three months isn't long."

"Maybe to a newt it is."

I know about things like newt lifespans, and I knew Mom was wrong. She knows I know that sort of thing, too, but she always has to say something positive. It's a disease with her. I picked up a good-looking rock to give to Charlotte (she's my best friend), and I got in the car.

Rodriguez had been a good newt. He'd done all the things a newt is supposed to do and more. I used to love to watch him swim, his orange belly glowing. He was graceful. And once I put my hand in the tank with my fingers spread, and he swam in and out of my fingers.

I rubbed the rock and wondered if I'd done anything to cause Rodriguez to die.

I hardly talked for the next hour.

Dad was too busy with the traffic to notice. But Mom did.

"Listen, Laurel," said Mom, "you've got to change your attitude. Heaven knows we've seen enough deaths with all your pets. And, sweetie, really, if you're going to be a veterinarian, you've got to get used to things like death." She glanced over at Arthur, who sat on the other side of the backseat with his forehead pressed against the window. "Arthur, what is that sticking out of your pocket?"

"Huh?" said Arthur.

"It's a corncob pipe. I can see it. Where did you get that corncob pipe?" Mom's voice had a worried edge. Arthur had been known to steal before. Mom called it taking without paying.

"I found it," said Arthur.

"Where?"

"In that shop."

Mom's voice rose in a little shriek. "You took it without paying?"

"I found it on the floor," said Arthur. I noticed he didn't say the bathroom floor.

"Oh," said Mom. Her face told all: She was trying hard to believe him.

"It's true," I said. I looked at Arthur meaningfully. Now he really owed me big.

"Well, you should have given it to the shop-keeper," said Mom. "He would have put it back on the shelf and sold it."

"No," said Arthur.

"What?" said Mom.

"He saw it in my hand, and when I told him I found it, he said I could keep it."

Likely story, I thought. But I kept my mouth shut. After all, I hadn't seen Arthur lie before, and it was interesting to discover he had hidden talents.

Mom twisted her mouth. "Hmmm."

"Mom?" said Arthur. "Is this silver?" Arthur held up the corncob pipe.

Mom looked at Arthur as though he were an idiot. Then she turned to me and accused me with her eyes.

It wasn't my fault. Sure, I used to teach Arthur all kinds of wrong things. When he was one, he loved to make machine noises. So I gave him my Yo-Yo and told him it was a special kind of car. He went around the house rolling the Yo-Yo and screaming, "Brrrooom, brrrooom." When guests were over, I'd say, "See how dumb my baby brother is?" And that was just the beginning. But I hadn't taught Arthur wrong things for a while now. I liked him a lot better these days.

Arthur asked, "Is it, Mom? Is this silver?"

Mom was still staring at me. She raised an eyebrow.

I shrugged.

Mom looked at Arthur and cleared her throat. "It's yellow and brown, Arthur. You know your colors."

"But the man said it was silver."

"The shopkeeper?"

"Yup. He said I could keep it as my silver ear."

Mom laughed. Dad laughed. Arthur's face got red.

I leaned over and touched his wrist. "It's a souvenir, not a silver ear. A souvenir is something you keep to remember something or someplace or whatever." I glared at the back of Mom's laughing head.

Arthur went back to pressing his forehead against the window.

I wondered why adults always think it's funny when kids get words wrong. Just the day before, I'd been explaining to Arthur about the old woman who lives next door to Aunt Lizzy. She stood in her yard, dressed with a bra on the outside of her clothes. We watched her pull the leaves off a bush while singing "Yankee Doodle." I told Arthur she had Old Timers' disease. Aunt Lizzy overheard, and lunch that day turned out to be nothing but a muffled laugh. All because I didn't know it was Alzheimer's disease. The laughing was muffled partly because Aunt Lizzy had a summer cold, but also because they had to laugh under their breaths since they didn't want to appear to be laughing at the old woman or at the disease, of course. But it didn't bother them one bit to be laughing at me. Even when my name for the disease made better sense.

Mom looked at me over her shoulder. I gave Arthur's wrist another defiant touch. She smiled at me. "It's good of you to be a sympathetic big sister, Laurel, but someday you're going to have to develop a sense of humor."

"How can she laugh when Rodriguez's body is barely cold yet?" said Dad. He likes to come to my defense. I didn't have the heart to tell him that Rodriguez was cold-blooded. Dead or alive, he was always cold. Anyway, Dad was right about one thing: I didn't feel much like laughing.

I pulled my sketchpad out of my backpack (I bring my pad and pencils just about everywhere I go) and drew Rodriguez with all the spots on his back, standing on the rock in his tank, ready to dive. I thought of how shrimp used to make him happy, so I put bunches of little shrimp in the water. After a while I looked out the window. I said, "The cows are lying down. It's going to rain."

Dad said, "It looks like a clear, sunny day to me."

Mom said, "I didn't realize this part of Virginia was so rural."

Arthur said, "Cows don't lie down."

I made a humphing noise and pointed.

Arthur followed my finger. He looked right at the cows and said, "Those must be sheep."

I went back to drawing.

Before we got to Washington, D.C., it had clouded over. By the time we hit Baltimore, it was pouring.

At the rest stop, Mom said to me, "You know about animals, all right."

"Yeah," I said, "that's why I couldn't even keep Rodriguez alive."

"Are you thinking it was your fault?" Mom put her arm around my shoulders. I shrugged her off. "You took excellent care of him, Laurel. Newts just don't live well in captivity."

Mom doesn't really know anything about newts, in or out of captivity. She just says things to make people feel better. But it worked anyway: I felt a little better about Rodriguez. I still missed him, though.

The next week, I sat in the orthodontist's office waiting to have my jaw expander checked. I'd already had that awful expander a year longer than Dr. Hayes had said I would because my jaw didn't seem to be growing.

A boy about my size came in and sat down beside me and said to his dad, "How many do you think will live?" His dad picked up an old magazine and flipped it open. The boy spoke louder. "How many, Dad, how many do you think will live?" He tugged at his dad's sleeve. "How many?"

"How many what?" I asked.

The boy looked at me. His dad looked at me.

Mom looked at me. I looked back at all of them. Then I stared at the boy.

"Rabbits," said the boy.

This was getting interesting. I pushed my glasses back up (they have a habit of sliding down my nose) and looked at the dad. "How many do you think will live?" I asked.

"Why . . . none of them, I suppose." The dad frowned and looked at me closely. "Do we know you?"

"No," I said.

"How did you know about the rabbits?" he asked.

"You just told me," I said.

The dad looked at Mom a moment, then turned back to his magazine.

"Are you raising rabbits?" I asked the boy.

"I'm raising these," he said. "My cat killed their mother and most of the litter." He looked at his dad. His dad kept reading. The boy looked back at me. "But three are still alive."

I sat up straight. "Are they wild or domesticated?"

"What?"

"Were they your rabbits before?"

"No, my cat Fluffy found them. They had a nest under the porch."

Fluffy. I bet if he had a dog, he'd name it Pooch. Yuck. "So what are you feeding them?"

"I put a carrot in their box."

"How old are they?" I asked.

"Dad says they can't be more than a couple of weeks."

A carrot for two-week-old rabbits. "Your dad's right," I said. "They're all going to die."

The boy looked at me with big eyes. His father looked at me, too. Worry crossed his face. Virginia, the receptionist, came over just then and led the boy into Dr. Hayes's office.

I looked at Mom.

She sucked her top lip inside her bottom teeth and looked back at me.

"Please," I said.

She looked around the room. But there was no escape. She looked back at me.

"Please," I whispered.

Mom nodded. "All right. I guess you need a new pet. In fact, I didn't even expect you to last this long." She sighed. "Yes, all right."

The boy came out of Dr. Hayes's office, and Virginia called his dad over to make another appointment. When the boy turned around, I was standing right behind him. "Hi," I said.

"Hi," said the boy.

"Can I have one of the baby rabbits?"

The dad leaned across the boy. "You can have them all."

"No," howled the boy. "She can have one. One, Dad."

"Okay, one," said the dad.

"All I want is one," I said.

The dad looked relieved as he gave Mom their address. We stopped at a grocery store to pick up an empty cardboard box, then drove right on over to their house. The whole way, I had to work at not wondering what the rabbits looked like. If I hadn't stopped myself, I would have grabbed my sketchpad and drawn rabbits. Lonely, motherless rabbits. But I didn't want to because then I'd get a picture in my head, and I might be disappointed when I actually saw the real rabbits. So I just sat in the car with a blank mind and promised myself that before I went to bed that night, I'd draw the rabbits as they really were.

The baby rabbits were small and sweet, and I

loved them immediately. They huddled together in a rabbit family pile, big-eyed and still and as dear as anything I'd ever seen in my life. The boy pointed at the one I could take. It was just the one I wanted. If someone had told me to imagine the most perfect baby rabbit in the world, I would have imagined just that rabbit. I put my rabbit in the box we had brought. Its body was limp. But its fur was soft and thick and gray. As I was leaving, I asked the boy, "What color is Fluffy?"

"Brown."

Brown? I'd never heard of a brown cat. "All brown?"

"And yellow."

Instantly I pictured Arthur's brown-and-yellow corncob pipe. "Silver Ear," I said.

"Silver ear," said the boy slowly.

"Silver Ear's the right name, not Fluffy." I nodded. "I really think you should think about that. Who knows what a cat named Silver Ear might amount to someday?"

As we drove home, I held the box on my lap and sang softly to my rabbit. What would I name him? An animal's name is so important. I wanted this rabbit to know how very fine he was. His fur was deep and seemed to absorb the sun—all gray like the Spanish moss hanging from the live oaks near Charleston.

Spanish Moss. Yes. It suited him.

I admired Spanish Moss's long hind legs and delicate little whiskers. I wanted very much to pet him. But I figured I better sing a lot first so he'd trust me. I turned over recipes in my head till I knew exactly what I'd feed him. Cheerios soaked in cream and honey to start. I would make this little rabbit grow big and strong and happy. I would take care of him through illness and health, through good weather and bad. This was my rabbit. I was about to tell him the wonderful recipe I'd made up, just to get his appetite whetted and all that, when suddenly he stretched out in a hard spasm. That was the last movement he ever made.

2

Bun Bun

Thirty dollars."

"But she's irregular," I said, not adding that it was precisely this irregularity that made me want her so much. "It costs less for irregulars, right?"

"Irregular?" The new salesgirl looked at me with annoyance on her face. I wouldn't even have gone to her, except she seemed to be the only one in the pet store this morning. She was young—a teenager, for sure. Didn't she understand what thirty dollars meant to a ten-year-old? She pursed her lips and ran the fingers of her right hand along her earring hoop. "There's nothing irregular about that bunny."

Bunny. The girl worked in a pet store, and she called rabbits *bunnies.* I sighed. I had to be patient with this one. "Look, she's got a nick in her ear."

"So what?"

"A rabbit's ear is the most important part," I said firmly. "You can't charge thirty dollars for a defective rabbit."

"You want a cheap rabbit, get the ten-dollar ones." She moved her fingers to her hair and picked at the scrunchie that held her ponytail in place. "They've been here for months. They've got to go."

That was exactly the point. The thirty-dollar rabbits were only six weeks old. They were child rabbits, and they were just the right age to raise with love and tenderness, so they'd turn out to be the right kind of pet. The kind you could hold on your lap and feed popcorn as you read a good book. The kind you could roll in the grass with on a warm spring day. That's exactly the kind of pet Spanish Moss would have been. And that's exactly the kind of pet I needed. If I took a ten-dollar rabbit that had been sitting in a cage long enough to make it hate all people, it would probably never learn to love and trust me.

"Listen," I said, "I've worked hard for these twenty-five dollars," which was only partially true. Once I'd made up my mind that I was going to get a rabbit, I'd told Mom. She didn't try to talk me out of it. After all, she'd been with me when Spanish Moss died, so she knew how awful it had been, and she'd been doing nice little things for me for the last few days to cheer me up. The only thing she said was that pet store rabbits cost a lot. So I said, "They don't cost any more than ten dollars."

"Ten dollars?" said Mom. "You're sure?"

I wasn't sure at all. I hadn't checked yet. But already I was worried the figure was a little low. "No more than fifteen."

Mom gave me fifteen dollars. "Go buy a rabbit."

"You'll pay for the cage?" I said, knowing she would. That had always been our arrangement. Mom paid an agreed-upon figure for the animal (however much she considered "reasonable") and bought it a cage or an aquarium or whatever it needed, and I did odd jobs to pay for the animal food.

Mom said, "Mmm-hmm. You bring it home first. Then I'll get the cage."

That sounds backward, and for most families it would be. But I hadn't always been lucky. Once I bought a boa constrictor, and I wanted to make sure it wouldn't get hungry on the way home in the cardboard box in the front basket of my bike. So I bought it a mouse to eat. Boa constrictors the size I bought eat one mouse a week. They swallow it whole and then just sit there and digest the big lump inside. I dumped the mouse in with the snake and pedaled furiously.

What I didn't know was that this particular snake had just been fed a mouse the day before. So he sat there, sleepy and full in the box, and ignored the mouse. But the mouse must have been kind of smart, because he didn't waste any time. He attacked the snake. He bit it in the neck over and over again. I didn't know about any of it. The road home is kind of bumpy, and I had to hold one hand on the top of the box to keep it from bouncing out of the basket, and I wasn't aware of any motion inside the box at all. Plus I had my helmet on, and I always feel kind of otherworldly in my helmet, so I get all worried about traffic, and I keep looking around at the passing cars. By the time I got home, the snake was dead.

Mom stood there with the huge glass aquarium she had bought for the snake and stared at me.

We put Killer Mouse in the aquarium for a while. He seemed lost in all that space.

Arthur hated him. He came by and shouted, "Murderer!" about once every half hour.

Dad didn't like him much either. He said, "We can't afford to feed a mouse that eats snakes." It wasn't worth objecting that it was my job to pay for the food—and that the mouse probably ate regular mouse food, too. It wasn't worth objecting, because Dad only said it to be clever. He didn't want an argument. He wanted a laugh. I never gave him one. So he always laughed at himself.

I really didn't want a mouse in the first place. I wanted a snake. But I no longer even wanted a snake. This experience had soured me on the idea. Plus Bianca, my parakeet, had squawked so fiercely at the sight of the dead snake that I knew she'd never forgive me if I brought home a live one. So I buried the boa constrictor, and I gave the mouse to Arthur's kindergarten class. (That was last year.) Arthur cursed me for that in his own kindergarten way. He put cooked oatmeal in my desk drawer.

And Mom took to reminding me about the huge, empty aquarium. But I solved that problem later when it became Rodriguez's tank.

Anyway, after that Mom didn't buy a home for my

pets until they had survived the first night in our house.

So there I was with Mom's fifteen dollars. I got ten more out of my dresser. Those ten dollars were a gift from my grandmother Nini for my last birthday. That was all the money I had in the world. Since I have to buy food for my animals, I spend every penny I make just about as fast as I make it. I figured that with twenty-five dollars in my pocket, I could pay for the rabbit plus get plenty of food to start.

I stood my ground in the pet store now and didn't blink. Ever since Spanish Moss died, my hands had felt empty. They ached to touch another warm, furry rabbit. I would be a good rabbit owner. I would do my very best. This salesgirl had to sell me that little female rabbit for twenty-five dollars. She just had to.

The salesgirl looked over my shoulder. She dropped her hand from her hair and stood at attention. "We don't make reductions on animal prices," she said, but she wasn't speaking to me. She was looking behind me.

I followed her gaze and turned around to face the store manager. I knew him, Mr. Caldwell, because

I'd bought a lot of animals from this store over the years.

"Laurel," he said in his dry way, "are you trying to bargain for an animal again?"

It wasn't quite fair of Mr. Caldwell to ask it that way. He made it sound as though I was in the habit of bargaining for pets. Actually, I'd only bargained once before, when I bought my parakeet, and that was more than a year ago. Mr. Caldwell had been a hard-nose about it. But then Mom had given me an advance toward my birthday money from Nini (that was my ninth birthday), so I was able to buy Bianca anyway, even though she was the fancy, expensive kind.

Bianca was wonderful. She'd fly to me and sit on my head or shoulder. One day she was looking for me and I was in the shower, washing my hair, singing. Bianca flew into the bathroom and somehow made it around the shower curtain and slammed into the bathroom wall and fell—*splat*—into the tub. I took her out immediately and dried her off. And I put her in her cage and set it near the radiator in my bedroom. I sang her my friend Charlotte's and my favorite song till she fell asleep—the friendship song that goes, "If you're ever in a jam, here I am, here I am." But she caught cold anyway and died overnight. Even now, over a year later, it made me sad to remember. No other bird could be like Bianca.

But this was no time to be sad. I stood in the pet store now and looked Mr. Caldwell square in the face. "Sir, I know you don't like bargaining . . ."

"That's right," said Mr. Caldwell.

"But I need that rabbit," I said, pointing to the brown-and-white one with the nick in her ear. "I have only twenty-five dollars, and she costs thirty dollars, so . . ." I hesitated. "I guess you'll just have to give me a job for the remaining five dollars."

Mr. Caldwell's face registered surprise. Had he expected me to beg? Anyway, I could see from the way his eyes were scanning the store that he was trying to find me a job. I had said the right thing. I looked over at the rabbit that was destined to be mine, and I tried to give her a reassuring look. She yawned right then, and I could see her funny little rabbit teeth. I laughed.

"Jack hasn't shown up yet," said the salesgirl.

That brought Mr. Caldwell jumping to attention. "Jack's not here yet?"

"No. And I'm busy—someone's got to wait on the customers. And you're doing all the inventory. And"—the salesgirl gave Mr. Caldwell a knowing look—"it's not real nice back there." She tapped the fingers of her right hand against the palm of her left hand. She had orange nail polish.

Mr. Caldwell looked at me with a stony face. "There's no point in giving you a job that any of my employees would willingly do, right?"

I didn't like that question. I shrugged.

"A pet store has all kinds of jobs." Mr. Caldwell looked hard at me.

I knew things were about to go bad. I imagined myself helping to declaw a cat or holding down a boxer as Mr. Caldwell cut its tail off. What if it was worse than maiming? What if the missing Jack's job was defective-pet executioner? What if I had to help kill some old, diseased parrot? I had to fight to keep myself from squirming under Mr. Caldwell's gaze.

"So you can wash out the dog kennels. How does that sound?"

Relief flooded my soul. "Fine," I sang.

Mr. Caldwell looked at me as though I was goofy. "You understand what that means?" he said. "You'll have to make sure every bit of the stuff is off the bottom bars. We use a brush after we've hosed off the loose pieces."

Stuff. Was he using such a silly word just because I was a girl? He could have said *excrement,* or if he couldn't deal with that, at least *waste.* I wanted to say, "Hey, Mr. Caldwell, I'm no stranger to that 'stuff.' " After all, I've had animals for the past six years. But I knew better. I nodded my head obediently.

Mr. Caldwell marched into the back room without further delay, and I marched right behind him, straight to the rear of the dog kennels. He quickly opened a kennel and led a spaniel into the waiting room to the side of the kennels. That's where prospective owners could meet their potential pets and get to know them a bit before signing on for adoption. He pointed out the hose to me and showed me the brush and the bucket. Then he closed the door to the waiting room, and I was suddenly alone— behind the open, dirty, smelly kennel.

I was quick about it. I put the hose on full blast and shot the bars sparkly clean. Then I used the brush, just to make sure. The kennels had been designed by someone with good sense: The floor slanted away under the bars, and the water ran

down into an open drain. I turned off the hose and knocked on the waiting room door. "Ready, Mr. Caldwell."

Mr. Caldwell opened the door. "That was pretty fast." He inspected the kennel while the spaniel strained at his leash. "Yes," he said suddenly. "Yes, indeed." He locked the spaniel into the kennel and opened the next one. A fox terrier went happily into the waiting room with Mr. Caldwell, and I repeated the job. There were six kennels, and I finished in less than a half hour.

Mr. Caldwell put the rabbit into a cardboard box himself, whistling merrily. I guessed right then that the job of cleaning the kennels would have fallen to Mr. Caldwell if I hadn't come along, given what a ditz the salesgirl was. And I also guessed that Mr. Caldwell probably hated "stuff." It was funny to think of a finicky pet store manager.

Mr. Caldwell handed me the box. "I suppose you need some food to get started."

I had been worrying about that, actually. I nodded.

"Well, you did a fine job today. You were fast and thorough." He picked up a three-pound bag of rabbit pellets, the smallest size they sold. "I believe you earned this as well."

"Thank you, Mr. Caldwell," I said. I put the bag of pellets on top of the box with my rabbit and walked out.

As I passed the cash register, the new salesgirl said, "Take good care of Bun Bun."

"Bun Bun? Her name's Era," I said, without glancing back. I'd been working my way through names the whole time I'd been cleaning kennels. Era was the perfect name for this rabbit.

"Nuh-uh," said the girl. "We all call her Bun Bun. It's her name. She knows it. You'll give her an identity crisis if you try to change it."

I looked quickly to see if the girl was trying to cause trouble on purpose. But she had turned her attention to sorting the dog biscuits in the bins on the sales counter.

I talked to the rabbit in a loud, cheerful voice as we bounced home through the streets on my bike. "You'll really like your new home. It's going to be fun. And I won't make you eat just these stinky little pellets. I'll give you all sorts of treats. And you'll get used to Arthur. He's bound to squeeze you too hard at first, but he'll catch on. He always does. Except for the time he broke the neck of Jake, the baby drake. But that was a long time ago." I went on like that, trying to put the rabbit at ease. Finally, finally, I dared to use her name. "Era? Era, do you like that name?" The rabbit didn't answer.

When I set the box on its side on the kitchen table and opened the top, the little rabbit hid in the corner and refused to even look out at me. "Era," I called softly. "Era, come on out."

Mom stood behind me with her arms folded across her chest. She didn't say anything.

Arthur came in just then and peered into the box. "Bunny," he said, "come on out, Bunny." He smiled. "It's pretty. I hope this one lasts."

"Of course she'll last," I said quickly.

Arthur kept his eyes on the rabbit and tapped his fingers on the table. "Come on, Bun Bun."

I couldn't believe my ears.

And, amazingly enough, the rabbit came hopping out of the box.

"No," I yelped. "Arthur, don't call her Bun Bun."

"Why not?"

"Bun Bun is way too common a name. Her name is Era, not Bun Bun."

"Then why'd she come when I called her Bun Bun?"

"It was chance," I said. "Dumb luck." I looked at Mom. "Right, Mom?"

"I don't know," said Mom. "Some of us are more conventional than others. Maybe this rabbit would like a nice, normal name."

I wanted to argue. I even opened my mouth in preparation. But Mom's words sounded right. After all, the rabbit had come when Arthur called her. I felt a little sad. My rabbit's name wouldn't be beautiful and mysterious. It would be a name anyone could guess at. Bun Bun. I wondered if my rabbit would turn out to be just as predictable as her name.

She looked at me suddenly and did a little hop sideways. Then she yawned, just like she'd yawned in the pet store. I laughed. What's in a name, after all? Bun Bun held plenty of surprises for me, I was sure. Plenty.

3

Singin' in the Rain

If my mother finds out, we're dead meat." I was on the phone with my best friend, Charlotte, who was about to drive her mother up a wall. Charlotte never intended to drive her mother up a wall, but it always happened. Her voice dropped to a whisper. I had to press the telephone hard to my ear to hear her next words. "What do you think everyone would do if we both showed up in school tomorrow with red hair?"

"Both?" I jumped up from the table and looked around the kitchen, although I knew very well that Bun Bun and I were the only ones at home. I peered out the window to the driveway. It was pouring, and big puddles had formed in the low spots in front of the garage. Mom's car was nowhere in sight. She was probably still at Thom McAn's, arguing with Arthur over sneakers. Dad was at work. I lowered my voice anyway. I wasn't worried that if Mom overheard, she'd forbid me to do it. Mom let me lead my own life about things like that. I was worried that if Mom overheard, she'd laugh at me. "Listen, Charlotte, I never said I'd dye my hair with you." But despite my words, I could already feel a tickle of excitement.

"Come on, Laurel. There's not a single redhead in our class this year. We could be special. Everyone would notice."

Everyone would notice, all right. I had dark olive skin. There were no redheads anywhere in my family. "I'd look awful with red hair, Charlotte. You're the one with the right skin and eyes to go with red hair."

"Any skin and eyes go with red hair. Red hair is a statement!"

"It's your statement, not mine," I said. But I held up my milk glass and tried to find my reflection in it. I wondered what I'd look like as a redhead. I could see nothing in my glass but milk.

Bun Bun was now banging against the barricade

of Arthur's blocks, which were supposed to keep her from escaping the kitchen. As I stood watching, she managed to hop to the top and over. "I've got to go. Bun Bun just escaped."

"Look, your mother lets you do anything. So we'll do it at your house."

"No." I strained my ear for the sounds of gnawing. The last time—the only time—Bun Bun had managed to make it into the living room, she'd left her mark on a leg of the coffee table. Mom wasn't amused. "Really, I've got to go."

"I'm coming over right now."

"It's pouring, Charlotte."

"I'll be there in five minutes." She hung up.

It was easy to find Bun Bun. She never came when I called, no matter how sweetly I sang to her. But when I'd leave her barricaded in the kitchen, she'd go straight under the onion bin, the only thing made of wood. She loved wood. Now I headed right for the coffee table in the living room, and there was Bun Bun, happily gnawing away. I caught her after a wild chase around the furniture. "Listen, Buns, Charlotte is coming over."

Bun Bun sat in my arms and looked right at my face. She wiggled her whiskers.

"Don't pee on her this time," I said. "She threatened never to pick you up again if you do."

Bun Bun gazed at me in silence. Rabbits are quiet folk.

The doorbell rang. I opened the door to a drenched Charlotte. "Why didn't you wear a raincoat?"

"My mother still hasn't bought me a new one. I wouldn't be caught dead in a raincoat with dolphins all over it." Charlotte stepped in as she talked and stood dripping in the foyer. I remembered how envious I'd been when Charlotte had gotten that raincoat. I wanted a raincoat with laughing dolphins on it. At least, I did last year. Charlotte shook the rain from her hair and eyed Bun Bun with disapproval. Then she opened the totally soggy brown paper bag in her hand. "Ta da!" She pulled out a plastic bottle.

I read the label. "It's really shampoo," I said.

"Shampoo with a dye. We wouldn't want the permanent kind. This kind wears out pretty fast." Charlotte gave a smile that showed how pleased she was with herself. "That way, if we don't like it, we're not stuck forever."

I stroked Bun Bun.

"So let's go." She held the bottle out in front of

her chest like a flag and started up the stairs. "To the shower," she said.

"Charlotte, we can't."

She stopped dead in her tracks. "What?"

"I won't."

Charlotte looked at me, and her face got red with quick anger. She has that very white skin that really would go great with red hair. But it mottles up in an ugly way when she's mad. "I came all the way over here in the rain, and now you change your mind?"

"I never told you to come."

"Let's not get picky about it."

"Anyway, Charlotte, even if I wanted to, we couldn't."

"Why not?"

" 'Cause of my mom."

"Your mom?" Charlotte marched back down the stairs and stuck her face in mine. "Who are you kidding? Your mother never says no to anything."

"Not to me, she doesn't. But I know just what she'd say if she were here now." And I did. I could hear Mom's words in my head.

Charlotte didn't budge. "What would she say?"

"The same thing she said the time you had dinner

here, and you wanted wine in your water like me. She'd say we had to call your mom and get permission. She won't let you break your mom's rules in our house."

Charlotte turned the bottle over in her hands. "Your mom isn't here, Laurel. And we never asked her. And my mom never told me any rules about dying hair. So let's just go ahead and do it fast before your mom gets home."

"No," I said.

Charlotte sighed. "And I was going to tell you something important, too."

"What?"

"Something about that stupid bunny of yours."

I'd never liked Charlotte's disregard for my animals, but I had to face it: Some people just didn't understand animals. "Tell me."

"I'm mad at you now."

"Please."

Charlotte turned to me. "Oh, all right. I found a mate for that creature."

Happiness welled up in me. I hugged Charlotte and by accident squished Bun Bun so hard that she scratched her way out of my arms and hopped quickly back to the kitchen. I'd been trying to locate a male for the past two weeks, ever since school had started. "Whose is it?"

"My cousin's."

"Your cousin?" As far as I knew, Charlotte had only one cousin, and I'd met him several times. I felt very uncertain. "Your cousin Eric?"

"Yup."

"The three-year-old that whines nonstop?"

Charlotte grinned. "He's four now."

"But Eric lives in New York," I said. "Come on, Charlotte; that doesn't help at all."

"He's coming for Thanksgiving," said Charlotte. "And I got him to promise he'd bring the rabbit."

"Can we count on him? I mean, you think he understands a promise?"

"Of course he understands a promise," said Charlotte.

I thought about it. We had bought Bun Bun in the end of June. She was six weeks old then. It was now mid-September, and she was a full four months old. By the time Thanksgiving rolled around, she'd be six months old and the perfect age for mating. It wasn't good to wait much past that. Females who mate for the first time after they're a year old sometimes never take to breeding.

"There's a catch, though," said Charlotte. "I told Eric we'd play with him the whole time he was here if he brought it."

I groaned. I wanted to say, "How could you?" but, in fact, I realized Charlotte's sacrifice. "You did that for me?"

"What are friends for?" said Charlotte.

Her words were pointed. I could see by the way she said them and her stance right then that she wanted me to chew them over. She had her hands nonchalantly in her pockets—but really, there's nothing nonchalant about shoving your hands into totally soaked shorts pockets. "Well?" she said.

I looked her straight in the eye. If Charlotte was a good enough friend to ruin her Thanksgiving playing with Eric, then I could certainly be a good enough friend to dye my hair with her. "Okay, Charlotte. I have an idea, too." I went into the kitchen to check. Sure enough, Bun Bun was safely under the onion bin, gnawing to her heart's content. I fixed the block barricade so she couldn't hop over again. Then I went back to Charlotte, who was watching me from the hall.

"We could dye the bunny, too," said Charlotte.

I wished Charlotte understood animals enough to

know that dying one was a bad idea. "Bun Bun can't get that wet," I said. "It would probably give her pneumonia." I smiled to let Charlotte know that I knew she was bending over backward to be nice. "Thanks anyway." I rubbed my hands on my shorts as a gesture of readiness. "Let's do it outside." I walked out the door into the warm September rain, which hadn't let up one bit.

Charlotte smiled and followed me, silent and content.

I led her down the street and around back of the old stone church. No one could see us there because of the high hedges. I took the bottle from her and read the directions aloud. "Use like ordinary shampoo." I lathered up my hair.

Charlotte laughed in delight. "An outdoor shower."

"And on neutral turf," I said, spitting out rainwater. It wasn't my house, so I wasn't responsible for Charlotte's actions.

Charlotte lathered up. Then suddenly she poured the whole rest of the bottle on her hair.

"You're crazy," I half shouted as I watched the foam run down her face. "You're totally crazy."

"I just want to be sure," said Charlotte. Bubbles

came out of her mouth as she spoke. "Anyway, you're crazier. You want a houseful of hairy rodents."

I laughed at the thought of baby rabbits hopping all through the house.

It took about five minutes of standing there, belting out "Singin' in the Rain," for the shampoo to rinse all the way out of my hair. It took another twenty before Charlotte's hair finally stopped bubbling. We were hoarse by the end. And Charlotte's white shirt was now pink with hair dye.

Charlotte chewed on her bottom lip and rubbed at the pink stains. They didn't seem to be coming out. "Next time I'll follow the directions." She rubbed harder. "My mom'll go ballistic when she sees this."

I put my arm around Charlotte's shoulders. "It doesn't show that much. She probably won't notice."

"She'll notice." Then Charlotte lifted her chin. "But red hair's worth it."

As we walked back home, the rain slowed down a bit. I could see Mom's car in the open garage. "Maybe we can get Arthur to play with Eric at Thanksgiving," I said.

"After Eric bit him?" said Charlotte.

"He's a forgiving soul," I said, wondering how I could force Arthur into it.

We detoured up my neighbors' driveway to dispose of the shampoo bottle in their garbage can. Drenched as I was, I was happy. Bun Bun was going to get a mate. Charlotte was right: Whatever our mothers' reactions might be to our shampoo escapade, it was worth it. Baby rabbits were worth anything.

I waved to Charlotte. Then we each went home separately. There was no point in either of us having to face more than one mother.

4

Buster

The idea of breeding rabbits had come suddenly. One day I was drawing Bun Bun sitting alone in the corner of my room, and I thought of Spanish Moss in his rabbit family pile. I knew instantly that I wanted to have a pile of rabbits in that corner. I wanted to breed Bun Bun.

Yet somehow when Charlotte announced she had located a male, the day we dyed our hair, I felt a surge of disbelief. (And, oh yes, after Charlotte's hair dried, it looked pinkish for about a week. She stood around in the sun saying she had strawberry highlights, until it faded to her normal blond. But my hair stayed as chocolate as ever. My mom took the whole thing in stride. Charlotte's mom grounded her for a week—mainly because of her shirt.) Anyway, the news seemed unreal. I was thrilled, of course. But I didn't actually expect that my plan could work out just like that—effortlessly. Even when Charlotte reassured me that she had reminded Eric twice on the phone to bring his rabbit, I was positive I'd never set my eyes on him. So on the Wednesday night before Thanksgiving, I sat by the window in the living room and looked out on our lit-up front walk with a sense of foreboding: Eric would never show.

Dad sat on the couch behind me with his eyes closed, listening to Mozart. Arthur was who-knows-where. And Mom was upstairs on the phone. For as long as I could remember, our grandmother Nini would spend Christmas with us and Thanksgiving with Aunt Lizzy in South Carolina. So now Mom was talking to Nini, and after that she would talk to Aunt Lizzy. Then Arthur and I would be called to the phone, and we'd each say a few words to Nini, then to Aunt Lizzy. It was a ritual. I kept my ears open for Mom's voice as I settled myself down for what I expected to be a long, fruitless wait.

But within minutes, there was Charlotte, walking up to the door with one hand flying as she talked and the other hand spread out on top of Eric's head. I opened the door. "Did you bring your rabbit, Eric?" I said.

Charlotte bobbed her head and answered for him. "He sure did. And Buster is gigantic."

So Eric's rabbit was named Buster. I tried not to show my distaste. After all, Eric is only four, so he can be excused. They came into the foyer, and I shut the door behind them, pulling them inside quickly.

Charlotte's news worried me. Bun Bun was a dwarf rabbit. That's the only kind Mr. Caldwell's pet shop sells, and Mr. Caldwell's pet shop is the only pet shop I can ride my bike to. The book I'd read from cover to cover, which was supposed to give every detail necessary for breeding rabbits, said that it was preferable for the female to be larger than the male, so that he didn't crush her as they mated. But it didn't say that it wouldn't work if the male was larger. And big dogs and little dogs mate all the time. So we had to give it a try, at least. And I'd just make sure nothing bad happened to Bun Bun.

Eric danced from foot to foot. Charlotte let her hand fall off his head. He quickly picked it up and put it back.

Arthur came from around the corner in his pajamas. He stood halfway behind me and looked out from a position of safety. "Hi, Eric."

"Eric doesn't bite anymore," said Charlotte.

I looked at Eric. He was staring at Arthur. Arthur cleared his throat and asked, "When are you leaving, Eric?"

"He just got here," said Charlotte.

I spoke up. "He means, how long are you staying, Eric?"

Charlotte patted his hair with the hand that seemed magnetized to his head and spoke for him again. "Until Saturday morning."

"Then I guess we'll have to get to work first thing tomorrow morning."

"First thing?" Charlotte's face turned mottled pink with emotion. "Tomorrow is our first day of vacation. I'm not getting up before ten."

"There should be three matings," I said in a businesslike voice. "And they should be eight hours apart." I calculated quickly. "If we did the first one at ten, we could do the second at six and the third at two."

Charlotte's expression stayed fixed. Then it suddenly dawned on her. "Two in the morning?"

I pretended like it was no big deal to get up at two in the morning. "With that schedule, Buster will have had every chance to build up his active sperms, and Bun Bun will have an excellent chance of getting impregnated."

"I'm not getting up at two A.M.," said Charlotte. Her cheeks were now totally red.

"We have to follow the directions in the book," I said. "Remember your pink shirt that used to be white?"

Charlotte's eyes opened wide. "That's not nice."

"Well, it's true. You said next time you'd follow directions."

Charlotte stood still as a statue. An angry statue. "Show me your book."

I was dumbfounded. "Where's your trust, Charlotte?"

"I want to read these famous directions for myself."

I went upstairs, with Arthur sticking right by my side. I guessed he wasn't putting a lot of stock in Charlotte's assurance that Eric no longer bit. The book was under my pillow. I brought it downstairs. We all sat in the living room, and I opened the book to the right section. Charlotte leaned over to read, which was hard, since Eric sat between us.

"Look," said Charlotte.

"Look where?" I said, pretending not to know what she was talking about.

"Right there. Four lines down from the top. It says, 'Eight hours is the optimal lapse time between matings.'"

"That's what I said." I tugged at the book.

"No, it's not," said Charlotte, holding the book fast. "And look lower. It says that up to twelve hours is fine. See?"

"We want the optimal," I said in my most logical voice. "If we're going to do something, let's do it right. Right?" But all the while I kept thinking about how Buster was gigantic and Bun Bun was a dwarf and how I wasn't following directions myself.

"Twelve hours is fine," said Charlotte to herself, wrinkling her brow. "That means if we mated them at noon tomorrow and again at eight tomorrow night, we could mate them again at eight the next morning." She scratched her head with her free hand. "I suppose I could get up at eight on Friday. Or you could do it by yourself."

"Charlotte, you're taking over, and this is my rabbit."

"And it's my sleep." She nodded her head. "Yup, I think we should mate them at two tomorrow afternoon, then again at ten tomorrow night, and then ten on Friday morning. There." She sat back with a smug look on her face. "That's better."

"Charlotte," I said in a wail. "Charlotte, that doesn't leave us any time for an extra chance if we need one."

"What are you talking about?"

"What if something goes wrong? We'll have to try again."

"What could go wrong?" asked Charlotte.

"Any number of things," I said. "Maybe Buster won't be interested."

"He'll be interested," said Charlotte. "And if he's not, what can we do? Dress Bun Bun up in a sexy outfit?" She giggled.

Arthur giggled, even though I was sure he didn't understand what we were talking about.

Eric sat straight-faced, staring at Arthur. He didn't see anything funny in the situation. I was starting to like this little boy.

"There are other things that could go wrong," I said.

"Like what?"

I sighed loudly. "Like Buster could get confused and not get on Bun Bun the right way."

Charlotte looked at me in surprise. "You mean they really do that?"

"They've been known to," I said.

Charlotte giggled again. "How stupid."

Arthur laughed a big belly laugh.

Eric stared at Arthur. Eric really was turning out to be nice. I liked him a lot.

"Listen, Charlotte. Plenty of other things could go wrong."

"Like what?" she said, as I knew she would.

"There's no point in telling you. You'll just make a joke of everything. I want us to start earlier, and that's that."

"How early?" said Charlotte, with an edge to her voice.

"Let's go back to your plan of noon and eight and then eight on Friday morning."

"Okay." Charlotte nodded. Then she looked at me solemnly. "There's something I should tell you about Buster."

"What?"

"He's . . . I think maybe he's kind of, well, messed up."

"What's wrong with him?" I asked with alarm.

"His ears."

I thought of the nick in Bun Bun's ear. I smiled. It was fitting that Bun Bun's mate should have something strange about his ears, too. Maybe he was the right mate for her. Oh, maybe this whole breeding thing would work after all. "What's wrong with them?"

With a look of sudden resolution, Charlotte stood up. "You'll see."

Eric popped up beside her, keeping Charlotte's hand on his head.

"Why is your hand on Eric's head?" I asked Charlotte.

"He wants it there," said Charlotte.

"Why?" I asked.

"I don't know," said Charlotte.

Arthur leaned around me from behind. "Eric, why do you want Charlotte's hand on your head?"

I looked at Eric. He hadn't said a word the whole time, and I wondered if he had taken a vow of silence, like that order of monks.

Eric stared at Arthur. "I like it."

After they'd left, Arthur and I went upstairs. Dad met us at the top of the stairs and put us to bed. Mom didn't come to give a kiss, even though I knew she was home. It felt strange. But Dad said she was upset, and she'd gone to bed already. I lay there feeling incomplete—like I feel whenever I lose something.

Then I remembered Arthur and I had never gotten our turn to talk on the phone to Nini and Aunt Lizzy. That felt strange, too.

Then I thought about rabbits again. I wondered what Eric's rabbit's ears looked like. And whether Bun Bun would like him. And what the babies would look like. It seemed like hours before I finally fell asleep.

At a quarter to twelve on Thursday, Arthur and I headed over to Charlotte's house. We wrapped Bun Bun in a thick towel, both to keep her warm and to keep her calm. Arthur carried her because I had to walk with my right hand on his head. Charlotte and I had divided the day. She had to play with Eric on Thursday and Friday mornings, and I had to play with him on Thursday and Friday afternoons. Morning was the shorter shift, because Charlotte woke up late. But I was happy with the deal, especially since I had gotten Arthur to agree to play with Eric for me. His price was that I had to walk around with my hand on his head whenever he asked. As luck would have it, I didn't have anything over Arthur at the time. The secret of his finding the corncob pipe on the bathroom floor of that shop in South Carolina no longer mattered, since he'd lost the pipe long ago.

Bun Bun was going to go into Buster's cage rather than him going into hers because females can get territorial and fight if a male enters their cage. But most males seem to welcome a female onto their turf. I brought along Dad's thick garden gloves so that if anything bad happened, I could grab Bun Bun out of the cage fast without getting bitten too hard.

Eric and Charlotte were waiting for us. We all went directly into Charlotte's garage, where Buster sat right by the door of his cage, as though he were waiting for us. He was the biggest lop-eared rabbit I'd ever seen. He was creamy tan all over with chocolate markings on all four paws. What a beauty!

Charlotte chewed at her bottom lip. "Are his floppy ears too awful?"

"His ears are perfect," I said. "He's a lop-ear. His

ears are supposed to be oversized and hang down like that."

"Oh." Charlotte smiled. "Oh, good." She laughed. "Will the babies have ears like that?"

"I don't know," I said. My book didn't say anything about that.

Eric opened Buster's cage, and Arthur put Bun Bun in.

I stood ready to snatch Bun Bun out. But she didn't seem to mind. And Buster lost no time. Within seconds I knew I was on the road to becoming a grandmother.

5

Sore Hands

There was no way of knowing for sure if Bun Bun was pregnant. The book said that if you put a female into a cage with a male a week after mating and if the female cowered in a corner and cried or else fought like mad, she was pregnant. If, instead, she accepted the male again, then she wasn't. But a week after mating, Buster was long gone, back in New York. I drew a picture of him and taped it in her cage so Bun Bun could look at it every day.

I studied Bun Bun, looking for any little thing that might be different about her, any sign that the mating might have worked. But she seemed the same. She was just as affectionate as ever, and she ate the same amount. I was careful to measure out her mix of Tasteeos (Cheerios cost too much for a rabbit, Mom says), puppy chow, and rabbit pellets, so I knew for sure that her appetite hadn't changed. (I made up the recipe for her daily mix by myself, and I was proud of it. It had all the essentials for a healthy rabbit. Or, rather, it had all the essentials you could pack into dried food. But, of course, she ate fresh food, too.)

I thought maybe Bun Bun was drinking extra. Especially since she was taking in so much salt. I'd attached a round salt lick to the side of her cage, right beside my drawing of Buster, and she'd licked it almost all away already.

Whatever, I decided we'd better all treat her as though she was pregnant, just in case. So I went in the basement and found some scrap wood and built her a nesting box, about twelve by fifteen inches and about five inches high on the sides. I threw in an old pair of Dad's boxer shorts from the rag pile. The book said she needed cloth for building a nest. Bun Bun ignored Dad's shorts (maybe they weren't such a great choice), so I added a pile of old leaves from sweeping out the garage. Bun Bun quickly ate up all the maple leaves she could find. But she sure didn't build anything that resembled a nest.

About two weeks after Thanksgiving, I was standing outside by Bun Bun's cage when Mom came home and called me to help her carry in the groceries. As I laid them out on the table, I set aside the bananas and the strawberries. Mom noticed right away. "What's on your mind, Laurel?"

"Pregnant rabbits like bananas," I said. "My book says so."

Mom looked over the bunch of bananas. She picked one with a bruise and broke it off. "Okay, but no more than half a banana a day." She put the rest of the bunch on top of the refrigerator, where we usually kept them. She looked at the strawberries. "Does your book say pregnant rabbits eat strawberries, too?"

"No. But when you were pregnant with Arthur, you ate tons of strawberries."

"You were only four years old then," said Mom. "I'm surprised you remember."

"I'll always remember," I said. "You shared them with me."

Mom laughed. "All right. I like the idea." She held out the basket. "Here. Two a day. And if she doesn't look like she loves them, stop."

I cut the banana in half and set the other half on

the windowsill for the next day. Then I went outside
and fed Bun Bun the half banana and the strawberries. She ate them all, every last bite, contentedly.

Each day was pretty much the same. I went to
school and raced home to check on Bun Bun. Did
she look fatter? Sometimes I was sure of it. But when
I held her, she didn't feel any fatter. Her fur thick-
ened, but that was probably just because winter was
coming. Julie, a kid in my class, had a birthday
party, and I snatched all the ribbons from her gifts
as she was about to throw them away. I figured
they'd give a festive air to a rabbit nest. (When we
still had Bianca, I used to cover the bottom of her
birdcage with wrapping paper whenever I could. It
made her more cheerful.) But the ribbons sat in Bun
Bun's nesting box untouched, and Bun Bun slept in
the corner of the cage that got the most sun—the
corner farthest from the nesting box.

On December 15, Bun Bun bit me. It was precisely three weeks after Thanksgiving, and I reached
in to take her out for her daily romp on the kitchen
floor, and she bit me. Just like that. Chomp. I
jumped in surprise, but fortunately I didn't drop her.
I put her back in the cage and sang her a song I'd
made up a long time ago about the wind. I used to

sing it to Arthur when he was little and got hurt so often. I thought maybe it would calm Bun Bun now.

Bun Bun hopped around the cage. I rubbed my sore hand and sang. Bun Bun jumped into the nesting box and did the strangest thing. She dug her head down under the leaves and tossed it up high, so that leaves fell all down her back. She acted frantic. I squeezed the bite on my hand and sang my heart out.

After a while, I went into the house. I figured I'd ask Mom what she thought about Bun Bun's leaf-tossing. But Mom was on the phone with Aunt Lizzy. Mom was on the phone a lot these days. And Dad wasn't home yet.

I knew my book hadn't said anything about this sort of behavior. Still, I looked again, just to be sure. Nothing. But I did notice the book was overdue at the library. I'd been checking it out for two-week intervals ever since September. Mrs. Lichtenberg, the librarian, said that could go on forever, as long as no one else requested the book. It was almost five o'clock, and it would be time to start helping in the kitchen soon, but there was just enough time to race down to the library on my bike and pay my fine and renew the book. So that's what I did.

The next day in gym I told Charlotte about Bun Bun's odd behavior with the leaves. I swooped my head down and tossed it back and arched my spine, so Charlotte could get a good sense of it. We were standing in line in a relay game, so there was plenty of room to do it right.

After the relay race (which my team lost), Mrs. Schachner blew her whistle. "Okay, everyone is going to be spot-checked for scoliosis today. Boys into the boys' locker room, girls into the girls' locker room. Shirts off once you get in there. Go."

At the words "Shirts off," giggles spread through the gym. The whole fifth grade was there, and what lay hidden under shirts was becoming pretty important to us. What lay hidden under my shirt wasn't anything to speak of yet, but Julie was already sprouting (as Dad says), and so were Kristen and Amy. I went into the locker room and huddled in line with Charlotte, our arms crossed tightly at our chests. When it was my turn, I bent over and let my body fall forward naturally, as the school nurse instructed.

"Stand up straight again, dear," she said.

I stood up straight.

"All right, now put your feet together like this."

I put my feet together like hers.

"Now stand tall and just relax and let your body fall forward from the waist."

I'd been in line for more than ten minutes, and I'd watched while the girls in front of me got tested. So I knew immediately that something was wrong. No one else had been asked to repeat the test. My chest tightened in worry. I didn't even know what scoliosis was, but I knew I didn't want it. I tried to relax. My cheek muscles twitched. I got a spasm through my shoulders. I let my body fall forward from the waist so fast that I stumbled and hit my head on the floor.

"Are you all right, dear?" The nurse held me by the elbow now and looked at the rapidly forming lump on my forehead.

"I just tripped." I looked around for Charlotte, but she had rushed off, like the other girls ahead of me in line, to grab her shirt and fly away happy and scoliosis-free.

"Well, you just sit down on this bench a minute, and I'll test you again in a bit."

So I sat, naked to the waist, humiliated, with a throbbing forehead, while the last three girls got tested. It was *zip zip zip* with them (as Mom says). Not a single one had to relax and try it again.

After I finally got tested again, the nurse scribbled something on a note and handed it to me. "Give this to your mother. She has to make an appointment with your pediatrician."

I folded the note carefully and put it in my pants pocket. I wanted to ask her the obvious question. But it wasn't worth it. I knew the answer.

When I went out into the hall, fully dressed now, Charlotte was waiting for me. She was solemn. She didn't ask anything (good old Charlotte), but just sidled up close to me. We walked together back to the classroom.

After the day was finally over, I was going down the school stairs, heading for the back door, when I passed Richard, a kid in my class.

Richard stopped right in front of me and looked at me with astonished eyes. "You used to be perfect, you know."

I didn't know what to say to that. I stared back at him with equal astonishment.

"Then you got that jaw-expander thing on your mouth in second grade and those glasses last year. And now you've got scurvy." He looked frightened by his own words. "You used to be perfect, just like me. And now look at you." He walked past me slowly. Then he ran the rest of the way up the stairs.

I don't like Richard. It's not that I dislike him; it's that he's never been anyone special in my life. So there was no reason for me to care what Richard thought or said. So there was no reason for me to fight tears all the way home.

I stood before Bun Bun's cage and dropped my backpack on the ground and reached in to pet her. She stayed quiet and looked at me. But when I moved my hand under her arms to try to pull her out, she gave me a quick nip. A warning. "Bun Bun," I said. "Don't you see I need you now?"

Bun Bun didn't say anything.

In fact, the only noises I'd ever heard from a rabbit were the little growly screams that Buster had made when he mated with Bun Bun. I wondered now if Bun Bun was a mute. Then she'd be disabled, like me. We could be a pair. Bun Bun jumped into her nesting box and threw leaves about in a frenzy. I wondered if she was going insane.

When Mom read the note from the nurse, she called Dr. Shy's office right away. Mom looked at me over the phone as she waited while the reception-ist checked in the appointment book on the other end of the phone line. "Are you worried?"

I nodded. It was a dumb question. I waited for Mom to tell me it would all be okay.

"I'm worried, too," she said.

I hadn't expected that. My stomach went cold.

Mom looked out the window and spoke as if to herself. "First Aunt Lizzy. Now you. What's next?"

"Does Aunt Lizzy have scoliosis?" I asked.

Mom looked at me, surprised. "Of course not." Then she turned her attention to the phone. "Yes. But that's too far off." Silence, as Mom listened. "No, I don't want Laurel waiting that long." Silence. Mom chewed at her lower lip. "Can I please talk with Rosemary?" Rosemary is Dr. Shy's first name. Mom sighed and half slumped. Then she straightened up suddenly. "Why, yes. We can do that. Fine. Thank you." She hung up. "Grab your homework. I'll get Arthur. Dr. Shy will see you this afternoon, but it could be a long wait."

And so we waited for Dr. Shy. Once Arthur finally decided to come out from under my hand (he'd made a habit of walking beside me with my hand on his head ever since Eric taught him that), he climbed about in the two-story toy house in the waiting room. It was for little kids, and Arthur was too big for it; he could hardly squeeze through the circular holes in the first-story walls. But at least he was happy. I wasn't. We waited some more. And then some more. Finally, Dr. Shy called me in and made me bend over. She used a little plastic thing to measure the curve of my back. It turned out that my upper back had a curve of 4.5 in one direction, and my lower back had a curve of 3 in the opposite direction.

"I'm not alarmed," said Dr. Shy as she had me lie down on the patient table. She pulled out an ordinary tape measure. "You shouldn't be, either." She measured my legs.

"What are you doing?" asked Mom, which was dumb, since Dr. Shy was clearly measuring my legs.

"If one leg is longer than the other, the back curves," said Dr. Shy. "It's a fairly common cause of scoliosis and an easily resolved one. But Laurel's legs are the same length." She measured my arms.

I wondered if Dr. Shy had gone insane, like Bun Bun. After all, I didn't walk on my hands, so there was no obvious way in which the length of my arms would affect my back. Unless maybe one arm longer than the other would mean I'd lean to one side and have a curved back. That could be it.

"Your arms are the same length, too," said Dr.

Shy. "Do you have a chin-up bar in your house?"

I looked at Mom. Dr. Shy really did seem crazy.

Mom shook her head at Dr. Shy.

"Well, if you want to, you might think of getting one. Sometimes hanging from a bar for a few minutes every day can help straighten the back. So long as your arms are the same length." Dr. Shy sat at the little desk in the corner and scribbled on my chart, then closed the folder. "All right, now, here's the story." She rolled her chair over closer to me. "The curvature is nothing to worry about now. But we'll keep a close eye on it. We'll test you every three months through your growth spurt."

"I'm not in a growth spurt," I blurted out. "My jaw's the same size it was in second grade."

Dr. Shy looked baffled, and I realized immediately that she never talked with Dr. Hayes, my orthodontist. But she didn't miss a beat. It was obvious she'd had a lot of experience dealing with kids who didn't make sense. "Well, you'll start spurting soon. So we'll just check regularly. If it gets to a five or six, then we can talk about a full-body X ray. But right now there's nothing to do but use good posture and take care of yourself generally."

I felt a little better driving home. I was only a 4.5, not a 5, whatever that meant. But how long did it normally take to progress to a 5? I should have asked that. Maybe I'd go to the library and get a book on scoliosis. I shut my eyes and imagined myself as a hunchback. My breath came hard. I opened my eyes. Dr. Shy had said I shouldn't get alarmed, and here I was, getting alarmed. That was dumb. Maybe for three months, till the next time I saw her, I should forget about it. Yes, that's what I'd do.

Only Dad wouldn't let me. After dinner he went out and bought a steel pipe. He mounted it in my door frame. "Five minutes a day," he said.

I hung for thirty-five seconds and dropped like a bag of wet sand.

"Not so good," said Dad. "Try again."

"I'd say it was good," said Mom.

"Try again," said Dad.

This time I hung for twenty-nine seconds. My hands hurt. First Bun Bun had taken to biting them. And now my dad was going to force me to wear all the skin off them.

I lay in bed that night and worked at not being alarmed. Suddenly I remembered Mom's words when she was on the phone with the doctor's office: "First Aunt Lizzy, now you." I thought of how often Mom had been on the phone with Aunt Lizzy lately and how little she laughed lately, and I got suddenly worried. First Aunt Lizzy, now me. I stared through the dark at the steel bar until I fell asleep.

6

Total Failure

Calluses form quickly. Within a week I was hanging from the new bar in my bedroom doorway for about two minutes at a stretch. It was good to have tough hands again. When I was little, I used to climb trees all the time, and my hands were always tough. I liked especially to climb the birch in our front yard—mainly because everyone would marvel that I could get myself up a tree with so few lower branches. But I gave up climbing when I got my glasses. The ground suddenly seemed much farther away. It shouldn't have, since I'm nearsighted and my glasses make things look closer, but it did. And I found I wasn't really crazy about heights.

Anyway, about that bar in my room, I had actually

come to like hanging from it. For one thing, it meant I was doing something to fight the enemy (the enemy was scoliosis). But beyond that, I could close my eyes when I hung there and pretend I was suspended somewhere exotic—the Amazon rainforest or the wilds of Southeast Asia. Hanging had turned out to be fun.

Now and then when I hung, I thought about what Mom had said about Aunt Lizzy. Or rather what she hadn't said. I asked her a few times, but I never got an answer. Mom was always just about to make a phone call, or already late for an appointment, or in the middle of balancing the checkbook. (I have a knack for bringing things up at the wrong time, Mom says.) Anyway, each time, she promised we'd talk about it later. But later she was busy. And pretty soon my worry got lost. After all, I had plenty of chores of my own.

My days were busy with getting all my Christmas presents ready. I was making Arthur an insect box. One side was a magnifying glass so that he could watch closely whatever he caught. I was making Mom a kaleidoscope from a plastic plumbing connection, aluminum foil, waxed paper, and a bunch of colored plastic beads. It worked good.

Dad was harder. He collects pigs—wooden, ceramic, glass, anything he can find. But I'd made him a clay pig for his birthday this year. So I decided to do a chore for him instead. I'd arrange all the firewood that now lay scattered about beside the garage into one long, neat stack. I had already begun on it, starting from the rear, which you couldn't see from the driveway. I was planning to finish it tonight, Christmas Eve, because I didn't want him seeing it early and knowing ahead of time.

Anyway, you get the idea: I was busy. But all the while I worked, I worried about Bun Bun. The book said that most rabbits give birth about thirty days after mating. It was now Saturday, December 24, thirty days after Thanksgiving, and I stood outside in front of Bun Bun's cage and looked for the tenth time at the empty nesting box. I slapped my bare hands together to warm them in the cold air, and I sang "Here Comes Santa Claus" to cheer up my rabbit, who lately had become decidedly fat. She didn't look cheered. I went inside, opened the Yellow Pages, and called the first veterinarian whose name I liked. It was a nicely musical name.

"Hello. May I please speak with Dr. Steinway?"

"The doctor is busy with a patient. Can I help you?"

The woman's voice was firm and older, and I felt I was talking to someone wise, so I decided to try. "My rabbit should be giving birth today, but there aren't any babies yet."

"Hmmm. Is this her first litter?"

"Yes."

"Hmmm. Are there any tiny feet in the nest box?"

"Tiny feet?"

"Sometimes they eat the babies. If they get nervous or upset."

"There are no tiny feet," I said, feeling sick. I knew that male rabbits often ate their own babies. That's why you always took the male away when the female was pregnant. But I had no idea that a mother would do it, too.

"Have you checked?"

I hadn't actually looked carefully enough to see tiny feet. But I had to end this line of questioning, so I lied. "Yes."

"How many days has it been since conception?"

"Thirty."

"Oh, well, there's your answer."

I felt stupid. "Huh?"

"A first litter can come anywhere from twenty-eight to thirty-five days after conception. If she doesn't give birth by, let's say, Tuesday, bring her in."

"Okay," I said. "Thank you."

"You're welcome." The voice hung up.

I went outside to tell Bun Bun, and I caught her ripping the fur out of her back with her teeth. I watched, fascinated, as she pulled a big, fluffy pile out from right above her tail. She was sitting in her nesting box, and she ignored me. When she had finished, she sat still in her quiet rabbit way.

"Soon," I whispered. Then I fed Bun Bun an extra strawberry.

The next day was Christmas. It was full of the wonderful things that Christmas is always full of, although now that I was big, my gifts weren't usually surprises. Just mainly clothes. But this Christmas was different from any other in one big way: Nini was missing. She had decided to spend Christmas with Aunt Lizzy.

"It isn't fair," said Arthur.

And it wasn't. "Nini already spent Thanksgiving with Aunt Lizzy," I said.

Mom sat on the couch and drank hot cider slowly.

"Aunt Lizzy needs Nini now more than we do."

"Why?" asked Arthur. It was exactly the question I wanted to ask. My old worry nagged at me.

Mom sighed. "She just does." Then she stood up. "Time to roll out the sugar cookies." She took Arthur by the hand, and I followed them into the kitchen.

I was surprised Arthur didn't make more of a fuss over Nini's not coming. When Nini was here, she read to him nonstop. And she tucked little treasures under our pillows. Bags of M&M's and bright plastic rulers and Band-Aids with dinosaurs on them. I was getting old for that sort of thing, but I missed it anyway. Why did Aunt Lizzy need Nini more than we did? Aunt Lizzy has no children. She never got married. She usually traveled at Christmas to faraway places. But she was at home this Christmas, and Nini was visiting her instead of us. I missed Nini. And Arthur did, too. And suddenly I knew Nini missed us just as much. She had to. Whatever made her go to Aunt Lizzy's now had to be important.

I stood across the kitchen table from Mom and thought of asking her all my questions. But something in her face stopped me. I knew she didn't want to talk about it right then.

"Get out the cookie cutters, would you, Laurel?" Mom patted Arthur on the head. "Let's have fun." Her words were happy, but I knew something was wrong. Mom was keeping something from us. I measured the flour in silence.

That afternoon Mom spent a long time on the phone with Nini and Aunt Lizzy again, just like on Thanksgiving. But at least this time Arthur and I got to say hi, too.

I had hoped that I'd get the best Christmas present of all—baby rabbits. But they didn't come. I fed Bun Bun an extra strawberry again, and then again on Monday. Each morning I searched through the nesting box carefully. No babies. But at least there were no tiny feet. Monday night I went to bed with the jitters. The next day would be the thirty-third. If there were no babies in the box in the morning, I had to take Bun Bun to the vet. What if it turned out the babies were too big because Buster was so much bigger than Bun Bun, and they couldn't get out? That scared me. I couldn't think about that or I'd cry. What if Bun Bun wasn't even pregnant? Boy, would I be embarrassed, bringing an empty rabbit in to the vet. But if she wasn't pregnant, why would she have pulled out all that fur? She hadn't shaped the fur at all, but I knew that the fluffy ball was her idea of a nest.

On Tuesday morning I rubbed a clean circle on the window near my bed and looked out through it. The grass gleamed with a slight frost, which was already evaporating away. I wanted to run downstairs and outside and look in the nest. But I was afraid. My fear kept me in bed about ten seconds.

Then I ran barefoot out to Bun Bun's cage. She sat near the door, far from the nesting box. I stared into the nesting box. The pile of fluff looked just the same. I looked back at Bun Bun. She stared at me and stepped into her food dish. She was hungry. I looked back at the fluff ball. It moved. Oh, did it really? I put my face right against the bars of the cage. The fluff ball moved again. My heart jumped. I opened the cage and reached my hand in. With just my index finger, I poked around through the rabbit-fur nest very gently. The babies were hot and soft and silky. If my finger was right, there were four of them.

I pulled my hand back and petted Bun Bun. She came to me for the first time in over a week. I lifted her out and hugged her, petting her all over. Her tummy was lined with hard, full nipples. She was thin again. I kissed her on the nose and put her into the nesting box. She jumped out and sat back in her food dish. I laughed. "You must be starving after all that work!"

I ran inside and came back with an extra large portion of rabbit mix and a whole banana. I watched her eat. She was ravenous. The fluff ball moved and moved, just tiny little stirrings. I was so happy, I wanted to sing to the world. I ran into the middle of the backyard, and I belted out "Frosty the Snow Man." We have tolerant neighbors (as Dad has often said to Mom after Arthur has done something that would have disturbed most neighbors), so I didn't hold myself back.

Mom leaned out the porch door. "Laurel, are you barefoot? And all you have on is your nightgown. Come inside right now."

I ran inside. "There are four of them," I said.

"Four?" Mom looked at me. Then a smile of delight spread across her face. She shuffled outside in her slippers and nightgown. I followed close on her heels. Mom stood by the cage door and looked at Bun Bun with a frown. "Why don't you go into the box, Bun Bun? Go nurse your babies."

Bun Bun didn't answer. She sat in the corner of the cage, far from the nesting box.

"They nurse only a few times a day," I said, reciting facts from my book. But deep inside I felt confused. Wasn't Bun Bun supposed to stay near her babies to protect them? But then, there was nothing to protect them from. They were perfectly safe in the cage. Maybe Bun Bun was smart enough to realize that.

Mom and I went back into the kitchen.

Mom sat down with a cup of coffee and stirred it thoughtfully. "Are you sure she's acting right?"

"How can I be?" I said.

"You didn't touch them, did you?"

My mouth went dry. I knew very well that if you touched a nest of eggs or even a baby bird, the mother might well abandon the nest. "Well, yes," I managed in a croaky voice. "I put my finger in. Just one finger."

Mom stared at her coffee. "Maybe that's why she won't go near them."

"Who won't go near who?" said Arthur, coming into the kitchen. He grabbed a box of Wheat Chex and set it on the table.

"Bun Bun won't go near her babies," said Mom.

"Baby bunnies!" shouted Arthur. He ran out the door in his pajamas.

I ran after him. "Don't you dare open that cage. Don't you touch them," I said frantically. "If anyone touches them, Bun Bun won't take care of them." Mom had to be wrong. Just touching them couldn't make Bun Bun stay away from them. Never. But no matter what, I wasn't going to take any chances. I wasn't going to let Arthur touch them.

Arthur stood with his face smashed up against the cage bars. "Where are they? I don't see them."

"Watch the fur nest," I said. "It moves sometimes."

Just then, as if on cue, the fur moved.

"Oooo," whispered Arthur. "What do they look like?"

"I don't know. I haven't seen them. But there's four of them."

"How do you know?" said Arthur.

Oh no. I was going to have to tell him. "I felt them with my finger."

Arthur stared at me. "Then Bun Bun won't take care of them."

"Yes, she will," I said. My voice cracked. "I'm an exception."

Arthur accepted that. He smiled at Bun Bun. "Good work, Bunny." He ran back inside.

I was starting to shiver. I'd spent most of the past half hour outside in 35-degree weather with nothing on but a flannel nightgown. "I'm going inside now, Bun Bun. No one will bother you. Please take care of your babies."

Bun Bun didn't budge. She had eaten about half of her mix and sat all bunched up in the corner. I picked her up and put her in the nesting box. She stuck her nose into the middle of the fur nest. I held my breath. She mustn't eat them. If she started to eat them, I'd grab her away fast. But Bun Bun didn't make any move to eat them. She twisted around and bit more fur out of her back and spit it onto the nest. Then she jumped out of the box.

When I got back inside the kitchen, Dad was having coffee with Mom. "How's she doing?" he said to me.

"She's still not in the nesting box," I said. "But she added fur to the nest."

"That sounds like a good sign," said Mom. She looked at me with sad eyes. I could tell she felt sorry she'd said it was my fault Bun Bun wasn't with her babies. "Have some cereal, Laurel."

"Later," I said. I went upstairs and got dressed. Then I sat on my bed, and I closed my eyes. *Please, please, let Bun Bun take care of her babies. Please, please, don't let me have ruined everything.* I looked over at my desk. The top of it was a cluttered mess. I spent a long time straightening it. Then I went downstairs and out to Bun Bun's cage. She was still sitting in the corner. I put her into the nesting box. She jumped out. I went upstairs and checked my book. It said nothing about this. I went downstairs and opened the Yellow Pages and dialed.

"Please, may I speak with Dr. Steinway?"

"The doctor is busy with a patient. Can I help you?" said the voice I recognized from last time.

"Oh, my rabbit just had babies," I said.

"Yes?"

My voice cracked as I said the terrible words. "And she's not going near them."

"What do you mean?"

"Well, the babies are in the nesting box, and the mother isn't," I said as matter-of-factly as I could. I didn't want to say it too complainingly. That would be disloyal to Bun Bun.

"Oh. Well, has she nursed them?"

"I don't know."

"How long ago did she have them?"

"I don't know. They weren't there last night when I went to bed, but there they were when I woke up." I looked at the clock. "That must have been around eight."

"Maybe she nursed them during the night."

I didn't know what to say to that. "Should I do anything?"

"Are you the little girl who called me a few days ago?"

"Yes," I said. "Should I do anything?"

"No, just leave it up to the mother rabbit."

"I . . . I . . . I did a bad thing," I said.

"A bad thing?"

"I touched the babies. I didn't know you weren't supposed to. My book didn't say that."

"Are you the mother rabbit's owner?"

"Yes," I said.

"And how long have you had her?"

"Since she was a baby. Since last summer."

"And do you touch her at all?"

"Of course," I said. "I play with her every day. I take her out, and we play on the kitchen floor. Only she stopped letting me pick her up a little while ago. But this morning she let me hold her again."

"Then you didn't do anything bad," said the voice on the phone. "As long as the mother rabbit trusts you, you can touch her babies. It's only if strangers or people she thinks are enemies touch them that you've got a problem. You didn't do anything bad."

She sounded like she was somebody's mother. I liked her a lot. "So what should I do now?"

"As long as the babies are safe in their nest, just let the mother do what she does. She did make a nest for them, didn't she?"

"Yes."

"Good. Well, good-bye now. Call us if there are any problems." She hung up.

I went outside and sat on the ground in the driveway and watched Bun Bun. She never went near the nesting box.

I called Charlotte with the news, and she came over at lunchtime. Her cousin Eric was in town again, and he had brought his rabbit, Buster, with him. Charlotte came alone to my house, thank heavens. But she told me that when Eric had heard Bun Bun had had babies, he wanted Buster to see them. I thought of bitten-off tiny feet and told Charlotte to tell Eric I'd cut his heart out if he brought Buster anywhere near the babies. (I learned from living with

Arthur that the more serious the threat is, the better little boys listen.) Charlotte stood with me by the cage in reverent silence, and we watched the fur nest move.

I spent most of the day watching that cage. Bun Bun never went in the nesting box, so far as I could see.

The next morning I ran downstairs early and hoped I'd catch Bun Bun in the act of nursing. Instead, she sat alone in her corner. I stared at the fur nest. My breath came in shallow, dry pants. My chest was so tight, it hurt. I waited for the nest to move. It had to move. It had to. I waited and waited. Finally, I reached in a finger and touched the four cold, stiff little bodies.

7

The Birch

Arthur and I stood silent as Dad buried the dead rabbits in the half-frozen ground. They looked like gray lumps with stumpy ears. I couldn't take my eyes off them. Even when they disappeared under the clumpy dirt, I stood staring at the spot where I'd last seen them. It was right beside Spanish Moss's grave.

"Come inside, Laurel." Mom put her hand on my shoulder.

"Not yet," I said. I heard them all go inside. Then I went to the middle of the backyard, and I sat down on the wet, cold grass. I looked at the ground for a long time. There were no little grass creatures in sight. All the ants and crickets and spiders were hibernating or dead. I closed my eyes and imagined the grass in the spring, with all its crawly life.

Arthur came outside and sat beside me. I knew it was him, even with my eyes closed, because he put my hand on his head. "What are you doing?" he said.

"Looking at the ground," I said.

"With your eyes closed?" said Arthur.

"Yes," I said.

"There's nothing there," said Arthur.

I opened my eyes and looked at him. He was squeezing his eyes shut. "Don't try so hard," I said.

Arthur opened his eyes. "I wish the bunnies weren't dead," he said. "I wish bunnies didn't have to die. I wish we didn't have to die."

"We can't help it," I said.

Arthur went back inside.

I went into the front yard and climbed up in the naked birch tree and lay flat on my stomach, draped over a wide branch. I hugged tight.

I knew the sky was dazzling and blue above me. I knew the dirt was hard and black below me. I knew the wind was bringing in much colder air. I love the weather. People always say the weather is boring. They say that if you talk about the weather, it's because you have nothing better to talk about. But that's not true.

The weather isn't boring at all. It brings the sun, from which all life comes. It brings the rain. It can make things live or die. It made this birch tree grow. And my tears, the ones flooding down my cheeks right now, would make this birch grow even taller. I wanted it to grow forever. I wanted it to touch the sky, then pierce it through and keep on going.

8

Answers

I'm sorry," said the woman whose voice I knew so well by now. "That's terrible. Yes, let me get the doctor."

I waited, half amazed. It was New Year's Eve, and Dr. Steinway and his helper were in the office. They'd been there on Christmas Eve, too, the last time I called. Veterinarians are dedicated people. I'd wanted to call Dr. Steinway right away on Wednesday morning. In some vague way I think I hoped he could take those cold little bodies and breathe life back into them. But I could hardly speak. And then Dad was so quick and efficient about burying them. Our pet cemetery was growing.

I clutched the phone with nervous hands. For three days I'd been thinking things through. In a very secret way I was angry at Dr. Steinway. If he had come to the phone himself last time I called, maybe the babies would still be alive. I knew this anger was irrational, and I kept it well hidden as I talked to the helper. But I was determined to find out what went wrong. I needed an answer.

"All of them died, huh?" Dr. Steinway's voice made me jump. He cleared his throat. His voice was gruff, as though he were very old.

"Yes," I said.

"This happens now and then. It's not typical. But it does happen. A mother just won't get the idea the first time around. Did her milk come in?"

"I think so," I said.

"But she didn't feed them?"

"I don't think so," I said.

"And they were warm?"

"The cage is outside. . . ."

"Outside? The cage is outside in this weather?"

"Well, yes," I said. I swallowed the lump in my throat. "The cage is in a corner, protected from the wind, but it's outside."

"If she wasn't sitting on them, keeping them warm, then they'd have died from exposure even if she nursed them," said Dr. Steinway.

"Oh," I said. Oh, maybe they would have lived if I had taken them inside. Oh, I was so stupid. I could have easily taken them inside. My eyes burned. I blinked hard.

"Okay, now, here's what you do. You still have the male available?"

"The male?" I said stupidly.

"The father," said Dr. Steinway.

"Well, yes, actually," I said. Eric was in town, and so was Buster.

"Then mate her again. There's very little chance she'll abandon a second litter."

"Oh." I could feel the excitement rising. I'd have a second chance. And this time it would work. "How long should I wait?"

"She had them Tuesday, you say?"

"Yes," I said. That's what I had told his helper. She obviously had filled him in on all the facts.

"It's Saturday. Usually we say to wait a week, but it really isn't necessary. She's a healthy rabbit, you say?"

"Yes, she's healthy," I said.

"Then mate her and call me when she's due. We'll keep on top of it next time."

"Okay," I said. "Thank you."

"Good luck, young lady." Dr. Steinway hung up.

I telephoned Charlotte. Fifteen minutes later, Arthur and I were standing at Charlotte's front door with Bun Bun wrapped in a towel in Arthur's arms and my right hand on Arthur's head.

Charlotte opened the door. "You're lucky," she said. "Buster leaves tomorrow afternoon. There's just enough time for three matings."

Arthur and I went inside. Buster was in a cage in the entranceway, just waiting for Bun Bun. Eric stood in front of the cage.

"Why does she have her hand on your head?" said Eric to Arthur.

Arthur looked at Eric as though he were crazy. "I like it," he said. He came closer and gave Eric a probing look. "You used to like it, too," he said.

Eric's face brightened. "Oh, yeah. I forgot." Eric opened the cage door.

Arthur put Bun Bun into the cage.

Buster went to work.

"Want to race?" said Eric to Arthur.

Arthur looked around. "Here, in the hall?"

"Sure."

"Okay," said Arthur.

"Ready, go," said Eric.

They both ran. Arthur was ahead in a flash.

"Hey, no fair," said Eric. "You're faster."

"Oh," said Arthur. He looked confused.

"Let's do it again," said Eric. "But this time don't get ahead of me. It's not fair."

"Okay," said Arthur.

I looked over at Charlotte. She was struggling to hold in laughter.

"Why don't you go outside to race?" said Charlotte.

"Sure," said Arthur.

The boys went outside.

Charlotte burst out laughing.

"It wasn't that funny," I said. "Lots of things aren't fair." I thought of Nini not coming for Christmas. And I thought of Bun Bun's babies. "Lots of things."

Charlotte sobered up. "I know. How're you doing?" It was the same question she'd asked me every day since the babies died.

"Fine," I said. It was the same answer.

"Come on," said Charlotte.

I followed as she led me into the living room. There was a pillow on the floor near the wall. Charlotte knelt down and put the very top of her head on the pillow and then kicked up her legs and balanced them against the wall behind her. I stared at her.

"If you stand on your head," said Charlotte, her face getting redder by the second, "you'll be beautiful."

"What?" I gaped. I thought about Richard—and about my glasses and my jaw expander and my scoliosis. Would anyone ever think I was beautiful? "How can standing on your head make you beautiful?"

"I can't talk this way," said Charlotte in a barely comprehensible garble.

"Your face is like a beet," I said.

"Grrmmm," mumbled Charlotte.

"Your feet are turning blue," I said.

Charlotte let her feet down and sat on the floor. "How could you know my feet are turning blue? I have socks on."

"I guessed." I sat down beside her.

Charlotte smiled. "Anyway, it'll work."

"What will work?"

"Standing on your head makes your cheeks pink."

Charlotte rubbed her cheeks happily. "I'm going to look better than if I had makeup on."

"That's a lot of trouble for pink cheeks," I said. "You could just pinch your cheeks and they'd be pink."

"Pinching hurts. And that pink doesn't last. Anyway, standing on your head is good for your health. It's a circulation thing. For every minute you stand on your head," said Charlotte, "you add at least a minute and a half to your life."

"That can't be true," I said.

"It is."

I shook my head. "If it were true, that would mean that if you stood on your head, you'd never die."

"Huh?" said Charlotte.

"Well, see, anytime you thought you were about to die, all you'd have to do is stand on your head and you'd keep living. And that's ridiculous, of course. Everyone dies, whether they stand on their head or not."

Charlotte's cheeks, which had just come back to their natural color, were now reddening again. "Is death all you can talk about?"

"I wasn't talking about death. I was talking about how dumb it is to stand on your head. Your face was about to burst with all that blood."

"I like standing on my head," said Charlotte. She stood up. "I think Buster's done his thing. Maybe you should take Bun Bun home."

I got up, too. "Don't be mad, Charlotte. I'm sorry. Stand on your head all you want."

"I will," said Charlotte sharply. "My magazine says everyone needs to find the right answer for them. Well, standing on my head is a good answer for me."

"Answer to what?"

"To my beauty problems."

I looked at Charlotte's face. "I think you're pretty."

Charlotte's eyes softened. "Thanks." Then she looked away. She said softly, "I'm sorry they died, Laurel. I'm sorry for you."

I took Bun Bun out of the cage and wrapped her in the towel. Then I called to Arthur. But he had already arranged with Charlotte's mother to stay for the afternoon. So I went home with Bun Bun in my arms and no answer in my heart.

When I got home, I put Bun Bun in her cage and went in the back door. I found Mom slumped over the kitchen table with her head resting on her arms. There was a bowl of grapes on the table in front of her. At first I thought she was asleep. But she looked up at me as soon as I walked in. Her eyes were tired from crying. I could feel their heaviness. And more, I could feel my mother's misery. I sat beside her on the bench, close enough so that our arms touched. My shoulders hunched in dread. "What happened?"

Mom sighed. "I guess you have a right to know. Aunt Lizzy's sick."

As soon as she said it, I knew I'd known it all along. That's why we didn't get to talk to her at Thanksgiving. That's why Mom had been on the phone with her so much. That's why Nini went to her house for Christmas instead of ours. I looked at the calluses on my palms from hanging on the steel bar. Aunt Lizzy was sick. That's why Mom had said, "First Aunt Lizzy, now you." I picked a grape off the bunch in the bowl and rolled it around on the table. "What's the matter with her?"

"Remember that cold she had last summer? How it wouldn't go away?" Mom got up and opened the refrigerator. She got out the milk and poured me a glass. I hadn't asked for it, but I knew she needed me to drink it. Mom has to feed people when she's sad. I took a sip of milk. Mom sat back down. "It wasn't a cold. It was pneumonia. And when they checked her lungs out thoroughly, they found cancer."

Cancer. I knew the zodiac sign Cancer, and I had a sudden image of little crabs, thousands of little crabs, crawling about in Aunt Lizzy's chest, ripping away little bits of her lungs till there was nothing left. "Lung cancer. That isn't fair. Aunt Lizzy doesn't smoke."

"It's not actually lung cancer. It's cancer of the bronchial tubes. The tubes that carry the air into the lungs."

"Aunt Lizzy is a runner," I said stupidly. There's no reason why runners should have strong bronchial tubes. But I said it anyway. I said it like a challenge. I wanted to fight. I wanted someone to walk in so I could just take a flying tackle and knock the person to the ground. My glasses clouded over. I took them off and set them on the table.

Mom slid closer along the bench and put her arm around me. "Yes. She's a runner and she's got a strong heart and she's in perfect health." She gave a sad little laugh. "Except for the cancer. But they're giving her all sorts of chemotherapy. The latest things. Experimental drugs."

"So is she getting better?"

"It's too soon to tell."

"Oh."

"And the radiation burned her esophagus so much she's bleeding, so they had to put her in the hospital and feed her intravenously while she heals."

"She's in the hospital now?"

"Yes." Mom pulled my head against her chest. My ear was right over her heart, and I could hear the lovely, warm, regular thuds. She cupped my cheek with her hand. "I love you, Laurel."

"I love you, too, Mom."

"I've been thinking that I'd like to go visit her."

I sat up. "Go, Mom. I can do the laundry. And I'll take care of Arthur. And Dad and I can cook together. And . . ."

Mom laughed. "You don't have to do all the chores, Laurel. Just help everyone hold it together while I'm gone."

"Okay, Mom."

I helped Mom pack, and in the back of my mind was the picture of Charlotte, looking for an answer, her legs in the air, her face turning red, her feet blue as a cornflower under her white, white socks.

9

Second Chance

On January 22 I brought Bun Bun into the house and set up her cage in the basement. Our basement isn't finished like Charlotte's, but it's dry and warm, and there are windows on the side. I set the cage where the sun would fall on it all morning long. As I figured it, Bun Bun still had about one week left of gestation, but I wasn't going to take any chances. I'd bought a book on breeding rabbits. Mr. Caldwell had ordered a copy of it just for me. And he'd sold it to me at a discount. He'd finally come to think of me as a good customer—which only makes sense, since I was and always would be. The book said that no changes should be made in a rabbit's surroundings during the last few days of pregnancy or she might get nervous and abandon the babies or kill them. So that's why I had to move Bun Bun inside now—a full week before she gave birth.

It seemed strange to me that when animals got nervous, there was no telling what bizarre and self-destructive things they might do. It wasn't strange in the sense of unusual. I'd read a lot about insects and animals. I knew what happened to rats when they were put in overcrowded cages and things like that. But it was strange in the sense of illogical. When people get nervous, you can predict what they'll do. Arthur clutches for my hand. And these days he usually puts my hand quickly on his head. Or if he's around Mom, he'll get behind her skirt— even though he's six. And when I get nervous, I make myself busy. I build things. Like the sewing kit I made for Aunt Lizzy while Mom was gone that first week of January. We people do sensible things. But animals just lose it altogether.

"Are you going to lose it, Bun Bun?" I sat on the cement floor beside her cage and looked at her quiet face. "It would be fun to sit on a nest full of babies. They'd peek out, and you'd have to nudge them back."

The week dragged. On Tuesday Dad brought

home a bale of straw and put it in the basement. I added a good amount to one corner of Bun Bun's cage. She quickly made a tunnel through it.

On Wednesday I had my first three-month check-up for scoliosis. Dr. Shy said, "Exactly the same." She smiled, as though I should be proud of the news. I looked at the relief on Mom's face, and I swore to myself to step up the hanging. I had to beat the scoliosis. I had to make Mom happy.

When I came home from school on Friday, Bun Bun was busy ripping chunks of fur out of her back. "Mom," I called, as I raced through the house looking for her. She was in the upstairs hallway with Arthur on her lap and laundry clumped in piles around them.

"I'm learning how to fold everything," said Arthur. "That way if Mom visits Aunt Lizzy again, folding will be my job."

My stomach knotted. Had Mom received bad news? "Are you going away again now?"

Mom's eyes met mine. Her face begged me not to say anything Arthur didn't know already. Mom said Arthur was a worrier. So no one had told him Aunt Lizzy was sick. "It's just in case," Mom said. She smiled. "What's all the rush about?"

"Bun Bun's making a nest."

"Oh, great!" Arthur jumped off Mom's lap. "Let's go see it."

"There's nothing to see yet," I said. "Mom, last time she had her babies overnight. So could I, Mom, please, could I sleep in the basement tonight?"

Mom shook her head. "Sleeping on a cold cement floor is a bad idea, Laurel."

"I'll bring down the old mattress from the guest room."

"It'll get all dirty."

"I'll sweep the floor first. And I'll vacuum the mattress when I carry it back upstairs tomorrow."

Mom looked at me with "no" all over her face.

"Mom, please."

"Oh, Laurel." She pursed her lips. "You are really stubborn, Laurel. You know that?"

I smiled. "Thanks, Mom."

Arthur and I dragged the mattress from the guest room to the basement. He was silent. I knew he wanted to sleep down there with me, and I wanted him to. I'm not the type who gets frightened. Still, a partner in the basement would be welcome. I was surprised he hadn't asked Mom. We put a clean sheet on the mattress, and I brought down my heavy quilt.

Arthur was silent through dinner, too.

After dinner I got on my pajamas and went straight to the basement. I inspected the cage with my flashlight. No new family members yet. I sat on the mattress and wrapped my quilt around me and read *Julie of the Wolves* by the dim light of my flashlight. After a while, I put down the book. "Bun Bun, are you sad?"

Bun Bun hopped restlessly around the cage.

"Do you know your last babies died?" I got up and squatted beside the cage. "Are you afraid it'll happen again?" I opened the cage door and petted her on the head. She came close. "My mother's sister might die, Bun Bun. I'm afraid of that. I'm sad."

"What sister? Aunt Lizzy?"

I turned around and aimed my flashlight at the stairs.

Arthur stood on the bottom stair holding his stuffed kangaroo. He came over and sat on the mattress.

I don't usually give away secrets. I'm trustworthy.

This was just bad luck. I'd blown it. But I wasn't going to make it worse by telling Arthur some stupid lie. I shut Bun Bun's cage and sat down on the mattress beside Arthur. "I shouldn't have said that, Arthur. I was just worrying out loud."

"Is Aunt Lizzy dying?"

"No one says that. She's just sick."

"I don't want her to die."

"Neither do I."

Arthur took the flashlight from my hand and turned it on Bun Bun. "Is she going to have her babies tonight?"

"I hope so."

Arthur took my hand and put it on top of his head. "Let's stay up all night and watch."

"Does Mom know you're down here?"

"Don't be stupid, Laurel."

We sat in the dark, watching Bun Bun, who sat in the beam of light, watching us back.

I was exhausted, which meant that Arthur had to be ready to drop. "Listen, why don't you stretch out?"

Arthur looked around. "There's no pillow."

"You don't use pillows when you sleep in basements."

"Oh." Arthur stretched out on his back. I covered him with the quilt. Then he rolled over on his stomach. "Laurel?" Arthur rubbed his neck. Then he put his arms down straight at his sides. "Laurel?"

"What is it, Arthur?"

"It feels like chicken."

"Huh? What feels like chicken?"

"The sheet without a pillow. It feels just like chicken."

I knew I'd never understand what that meant. But I also knew Arthur was talking just because it felt so odd, sleeping down here. He was as tense as I was. I put my hand on his cheek. "That's good, Arthur," I said. "You like chicken. Now don't talk. Just sleep."

I woke up first, and the morning light was already flooding the cage. I crawled over and looked carefully at the fur nest. It moved. My grin spread from ear to ear. I wondered how many there were, but I wasn't about to reach in and touch them. I wouldn't make the same mistake twice, if, in fact, it had been a mistake.

I sat back on my heels in front of the cage until Arthur woke up. Then he kept watch while I ran upstairs and had breakfast. And that's how we did it: All day Arthur and I took turns watching. That was the only way to know for sure if Bun Bun was nursing the babies or not. But she never went near them. Not once.

By midafternoon I was beside myself. Mom had gone shopping, and Arthur was on duty with Bun Bun. I found Dad sitting at his computer. "I don't think she's going to take care of them."

Dad swiveled around in his chair to face me. "She's not nursing them?"

"No."

"Listen, Laurel. That's the way things are sometimes."

I shook my head. "It doesn't make sense, Dad."

"Lots of things don't make sense, Laurel; you know that better than most kids your age. You read about nature all the time."

"Nature would fall apart if all mothers acted like Bun Bun. Bun Bun should want to take care of her babies."

"Did I ever tell you about the summer I spent on a farm in Michigan when I was a boy?"

"Only a hundred times, Dad."

Dad smiled. "Did I tell you about the piglets?"

"Yes."

"All seventeen of them?"

"Seventeen! The sow had seventeen piglets?"

"Mmm-hmm. And she would flop down on her side, and they'd crawl all over each other to get to the nipples. Each piglet had his own nipple. Did you know that? Piglets always suck from the same nipple."

"Do rabbits do that?"

"I don't know. But pigs do."

"And the sow had seventeen nipples. Wow."

"No, she didn't. That's the point, Laurel. I don't know how many she had, eight or ten or maybe even twelve. But she sure didn't have seventeen."

My face went slack. "So what happened to the extra piglets?"

"They had to wait their turn. And then they had to scrounge around, hoping there'd be some milk left for them. But there were only a few drops left at most. And they got weaker and weaker."

"And they died," I said.

"Mmm-hmm."

"That's lousy!" I balled both my hands into fists and jammed them into my jeans pockets. "What kind of a world is this, where some of the piglets have to die!" I looked up at the ceiling over Dad's desk and blinked back my tears of rage. "All this stupid death. It's a terrible, rotten, lousy thing!"

"There's nothing you can do about it, Laurel."

"Oh, yes, there is." I stomped off to the kitchen and dialed as fast as I could. "Hello, may I please speak to Dr. Steinway?"

"That's me speaking."

"Dr. Steinway, I'm the girl with the rabbits. The ones that died because the mother didn't feed them. Or maybe because I had the cage outside. You remember me, don't you?"

"I remember you, young lady. Has your rabbit had another litter?"

"Yes, sir."

"And how're they doing?"

"She's not anywhere near them. And she hasn't been all day. We've been watching her since dawn, all day long; we haven't missed a minute. She doesn't go near them at all."

"When were they born?"

"Last night late. Or maybe early this morning. I fell asleep, so I don't know for sure."

"Well, it looks like we may have a problem on our hands, is that it?"

"I don't want the babies to die again."

Dr. Steinway's sigh came through loud and clear on the telephone. "Young lady, there's almost nothing a human can do to save those babies if the mother won't feed them. The colostrum—that special milk that comes in the first two days of nursing—will protect them from illness. If they don't get that, even if you manage to feed them, they'll be vulnerable to every germ around, and they'll never make it to a week old."

I felt doomed. "I can't just watch them die, Dr. Steinway."

"No, I suppose you can't."

"So what should I do?"

"Well, let's see here. She hasn't been near them since around six this morning or so, is that what you said?"

I hadn't said what time. And I wasn't sure what time I'd woken up. "It must have been around six or seven."

"Six or seven, you say. Okay, now first you give that mother a chance. You wait till seven or eight tonight at least before you interfere, hear me?"

"Yes."

"In the meantime, you come here to the veterinary

hospital and pick up a little plastic nurser bottle and some kitty formula."

"Okay."

"Yes. Well, I'll see you soon, young lady." Dr. Steinway hung up.

10

Bravery

Bun Bun didn't go near those babies. By eight o'clock Arthur was zonked because he hadn't slept all that well in the basement the night before. So he trotted off to bed. By nine o'clock I was fairly zonked myself. But I was determined to stay up and have my way. Mom wanted us to give Bun Bun till the morning. But I felt sure that if she didn't nurse the babies overnight, they'd be so weak in the morning that they'd just die, like the extra piglets. At 9:15 I made my decree: "Okay, that's it, folks. I'm feeding them."

Mom got up from the couch where she'd been reading the newspaper and went to the kitchen. I followed her. She opened the tiny four-ounce can of kitty formula and poured the contents into a sauce-pan. She heated it up. Then she filled the dolly-sized nursing bottle halfway and handed it to me. She didn't say anything.

We walked together down into the basement, and Mom turned on the bare overhead bulb. I reached into the fur nest and pulled out a rabbit. Bun Bun sniffed at the baby with interest; then she retreated to a corner of the cage.

The baby rolled over in my hand. It was no longer than an inch and a half, and its skin was light gray and silky to the touch. Its head was shaped like a long grape and was almost as big as the rest of its body. The ears were round, like mouse ears. The nose was flat on the flat little face. The eyes were shut tight. The tail was skinny and hairless, just like the rest of the rabbit. It was a complete little rabbit, just waiting for the chance to grow up. My heart beat hard. I would do everything I could to protect that baby rabbit.

I held it in my left hand and put the nipple of the bottle to its mouth. But the rabbit didn't eat. So I pushed the nipple under the edge of its mouth. But the rabbit didn't eat. So I forced the nipple into its mouth and gave the sides of the bottle a gentle squeeze. The baby's mouth filled with the yellowish, creamy formula. And suddenly it squirmed in my hand. Not a major thrashing about, but a firm, respectable little squirm. And it sucked at the nipple. I held the rabbit and the bottle for as long as his mouth moved. It was a long time. Finally he stopped. But he didn't just gradually stop. He stopped, and his head fell away from the nipple. "Oh, Mom, is he dead?"

We inspected the tiny body. It was all wet with the formula that had spilled out the sides of its mouth. But its chest moved up and down in regular breaths.

"I think he swooned with delight," said Mom.

I laughed.

Mom looked at her watch. "Laurel, it's nine forty-five. That one rabbit took a half hour!"

I held up the bottle and checked the level of the formula. "And he only ate half a teaspoonful."

"This is absurd." Mom rubbed at her bottom lip. "Okay, I'll get a couple of eyedroppers from the medicine cabinet, and Dad and I will help you."

Mom ran off and came back with Dad and two droppers full of formula. I had put baby number one on my lap, where it lay without moving, and I already had baby number two in my hands, sucking greedily away at the formula. Mom and Dad took babies number three and four.

Baby number two was faster and wilder. When he finished, he swooned away, too. And he was covered with sticky formula. I rolled him beside baby number one. Mom added baby number three. And we each took out another baby—babies number five and six. Baby number six was clearly the runt of the litter, but he made up for it with extra speedy eating.

"Your rabbits are fast," said Dad. His baby looked even more dwarfed than normal in his big hands. "But I think this guy's getting the hang of it." He nudged the baby with the nipple. It sucked weakly. Every few seconds Dad had to give it another nudge. When the rabbit finished, Dad reached in for another, but the nest was empty.

I put all six babies back in the fur nest, went upstairs, and fell into bed. I think I was asleep before I shut my eyes.

In the morning I woke up to find Arthur standing beside my bed, staring at me. "You're awake! Let's go."

We went down into the basement. Bun Bun greeted us and eagerly collected our pats. Then I reached into the nest and counted. There were five warm, furry bodies. The fur wasn't theirs—it was bits of the nest that stuck to their skins with the dried formula. My heart clutched. I felt around in the straw and finally found the sixth baby, cold and lifeless. Bun Bun let me take it away, as though it wasn't her concern at all. I didn't know whether she was too stupid to know what was happening, or if she simply understood there was no point in trying to keep a dead baby.

I held its body tenderly in both hands and brought it upstairs. It was all I could do to keep my voice steady as I said, "Dad, we've got one to bury."

"But five are alive," said Arthur solemnly.

"Five of them made it through the night?" Mom came into the living room holding a cup of coffee. "I'd have never thought they'd even make it this long."

Dad put on his hat. "I'll bury it."

"I'll help," I said.

"So will I," said Arthur.

We quickly got into a routine of feeding the babies three times a day: once when I first woke up, once when I got home from school, and once right before

I went to bed. It took a half hour to feed each baby, and they ate only a half teaspoon each. If I had done it by myself, it would have taken three hours to feed six babies just one feeding. But, of course, there were only five babies by Sunday morning. And, of course, I always had at least Arthur helping me, and often Mom, too. Dad wouldn't help anymore. He came and watched me feed them, and he was willing to hold the ones who were waiting to be fed. But he refused to feed them himself. I think he secretly feared that the first baby to die had been the one he had fed the first night. And I suspected he was right. But it wasn't his fault. That baby had been the weakest of the lot.

After every feeding, I went to my room and hung from the bar. I could hang for five minutes now. In a way, I believed that if I could heal my back, the babies would live. The idea was crazy, but I hung a little longer each time anyway. Sometimes I thought I could actually feel my spine getting straighter. It gave me hope.

And I vowed that every night before I went to bed, I would sketch those rabbits. That way I'd always remember them, how they grew and changed.

Sunday night a second baby was weak and listless.

I touched him and then I touched the others and immediately I knew: He was losing body heat. I held him extra long and rubbed his tummy to try to make him eat. But he didn't have the energy. By Monday morning he was dead. But the four others lived through Monday and seemed strong. I feared that maybe leaving the wet formula on them after they'd eaten had caused the second baby to get cold. So I brought down a dish towel, and after every messy feeding, I rubbed the babies gently but thoroughly. Then I took my index finger and rubbed them all over, top to bottom. I figured if Bun Bun had been taking care of them, she'd probably be licking them like that. I didn't know if it did anything for them, but it made me feel better just to be doing something.

On Tuesday morning the nest of rabbits was full of activity when I came down. They were used to the schedule, and they got hungry on time. Their bodies were covered in short, fine, gray hairs now. And their heads weren't so flat as before—in fact, their faces were starting to push forward around their noses. By Tuesday night, they had almost clear whiskers and miniature white front teeth on top and bottom. When we fed them, their legs thrashed in the air as though they were swimming. And when we put them back in the nest, those who hadn't eaten yet would lick the ones who had, in their frantic, blind search for food.

But one of them didn't eat well Tuesday night. And on Wednesday morning, he was too weak to eat at all. He died while I was at school.

The rabbits were now in their fifth day of life, and three of them were still alive. I kept remembering Dr. Steinway's words: Without their mother's colostrum, the babies wouldn't live past a week. Every day I tried to lure Bun Bun onto the nest. But she never went. Sometimes she showed a flicker of curiosity for these squirmy little creatures. But she never got close enough to touch them. Once I held Bun Bun in place and put one of the babies under her belly, hoping it would latch on to a nipple. But Bun Bun jumped out from under my hand and went to the corner of the cage, and the baby rolled away. Every day Charlotte asked me how they were and when she could come see them. And every day I gave her the list of who was still alive and told her she had to wait. Dr. Steinway had said the babies were vulnerable to all germs. I figured that the babies couldn't be isolated from my germs or Arthur's or anyone's in the family, but I'd protect them from everyone else's germs for as long as I could.

Wednesday night, the fourth baby died. I put a stone over his grave, just like I'd done for the other ones.

We had long since run out of kitty formula. But I read the ingredients on the can: evaporated milk, corn syrup, and egg solids. Then I telephoned Dr. Steinway and he approved my idea: I made my own formula, designed specifically for these rabbits. I separated an egg and poured the yolk in a cup. Then I added a can of evaporated milk and a teaspoon of maple syrup. I used maple syrup instead of corn syrup because Bun Bun loved maple leaves, and I thought maybe the taste might be inherited. The rabbits seemed to notice no difference. They ate with gusto.

The rabbits' eyes were still closed, but they were not just spots on their heads anymore. Now they were dark, protruding lumps. Tiny eyelashes had formed. And they had sharp toenails and long toes, which separated in excitement as they ate. Their back feet were longer now, and their back legs were getting meaty. When they stretched out to their full length, they went from the top to the bottom of

Mom's palm. They loved to eat, and the whole time Arthur fed them, he'd sing, "Yum yum yum, yum yum yum," in beats of three *yum*s at a time. He made us all laugh.

On Friday when I got home from school, I was looking forward to spending the weekend just playing with Binky (the smaller one—Arthur had named him) and Blossom (I had named her). We agreed that their names had to start with *B* since Bun Bun was their mother, and Buster was their father. But when we walked in the door together, we saw Mom's suitcase in the hall.

"I'm sorry." Mom came downstairs and looked at both of us. "I'm going to Aunt Lizzy's."

Arthur dropped his backpack on the floor. "Is Aunt Lizzy dying?" His eyes were full of tears already. He ran into Mom's arms.

Mom looked at me over Arthur's shoulder. I shrugged. There was nothing I could say. She knew how it had happened—I'd told her afterward.

"I'm going because I want to be with her. I miss her now." Mom pushed Arthur away from her at arm's length so she could look in his face. "I don't think she's dying. But if she is dying, I want to spend more time with her for that reason, too. You can understand that, can't you?"

"I want to come," said Arthur.

"This isn't a good time for her to be around noise and confusion, Arthur."

"I'm not noise and confusion."

"Oh, Arthur." Mom ran her fingers through his hair.

"Is she still having that problem with her esophagus?" I asked.

"No. The radiation's over. Now it's just the chemotherapy."

Arthur grabbed Mom's hand and held it on his head. "When are you coming back?"

Mom knelt down in front of him. "I'm coming back in one week, Arthur. That's all. I'll be home next Friday."

"One week is a long time," said Arthur.

We all drove Mom to the airport. That night we went to bed early.

On Saturday, Arthur and I played all morning. At lunchtime I made bacon, lettuce, and tomato sandwiches for Dad and Arthur and me.

Arthur inspected his sandwich. Then his face lit

up. "I know what these are," he said. "These are UFOs."

"What?" I said.

Dad looked at Arthur with furrowed brows and took a giant bite of his sandwich.

"You know. They call these sandwiches by the letters. They're UFOs."

Dad snorted, he was laughing so hard.

"They're BLTs, Arthur," I said, shooting Dad a dirty look. "UFOs are something else."

Arthur looked at his sandwich with embarrassment on his face. "BLTs. Oh yeah."

Dad managed to swallow his bite of sandwich. "This is a great lunch, Laurel. And both of you kids have been playing so nicely this morning, how about if we go to a movie this afternoon?"

"I'd like that," said Arthur.

I nodded. I knew Dad was trying to make up for laughing at Arthur's mistake. I guess that was the best he could do.

On Sunday, Binky and Blossom were nine days old. They had soft, thick fur all over, and it was mottled brown in some spots. Their eyes were still closed, but they managed to do a sort of flop-hop through the straw in the cage. Bun Bun seemed afraid of them. When they were awake, she crowded into a corner of the cage and wouldn't move.

But on the tenth morning, Arthur said the dreaded words. "There's something wrong with Binky."

"There's nothing wrong with Binky," I said.

Arthur held the rabbit in his lap and petted it gently. "He's half the size of Blossom."

"He's always been the runt," I said.

"He used to be just a little smaller. Now he's a lot smaller."

"But he's fat," I said.

"He looks sick."

I took the rabbit and laid him on his back in my hand. He thought he was about to be fed, and his legs beat the air in anticipation. His stomach was round as a tennis ball, but his head and legs were small and skinny. I brought him to Dad, who was setting out breakfast. "Look."

Dad put down the box of cereal and rubbed Binky's stomach. "It's tight as a drum," he said.

"What's wrong with him?"

"I think his system's backing up." He rubbed his nose. "I'm afraid he can't move his bowels, and his body isn't using the food you're feeding him."

"If I keep feeding him, do you think he'll explode?"

"Not actually explode, no. But I don't honestly know what will happen, Laurel."

"I'm staying home from school today," I said.

"You can't, Laurel. I've got to go to work, and you can't stay home alone all day long."

"Of course I can. I've stayed home alone before. And I've got to today, so I can call Dr. Steinway."

"No." Dad took Binky and cradled him in his hand. "I'll get Dr. Steinway on the phone. I'll do whatever he says. You're going to school, and when you come home, you'll take over."

"But, Dad . . ."

"No, Laurel. I'll write down everything the veterinarian says and leave the note here on the kitchen table. That's final, Laurel."

All day at school, I thought of Binky. He had to live. He was ten days old. He had come so far. And if Binky died, poor Blossom would be left all alone. Could a baby rabbit live in isolation? It wasn't natural. They were meant to be in large litters. Blossom might die from pure loneliness.

When Arthur and I got home, we ran to the basement. Blossom was balled up sleeping, and we couldn't find Binky anywhere. But when I picked up Blossom, there was Binky. He'd been under her warm body. He woke up easily, but he was sickly. He could hardly lift his head. I carried him upstairs, and Arthur carried Blossom. I read Dad's note on the table:

Dr. Steinway says it's a miracle they've lived this long. He says you should rub Binky's stomach and feed him, just like normal. I gave him his morning feeding.

Love, Dad

Arthur fed Blossom, and I tried to feed Binky. But Binky couldn't eat. I knew he wouldn't be able to eat, but I had to try. I held him in my hand till Dad came home, and I made Arthur hold Blossom. I figured that was the least I could do for Binky. Before I went to bed, Mom called. Dad spoke to her first.

Then Arthur got to have his say. Then it was my turn.

"Hi, Mom," I said.

"Hello, baby."

"How's Aunt Lizzy?"

"She's doing better, Laurel."

I hadn't heard that sort of upbeat talk out of Mom for a long time. Could it really be true? "What do you mean?"

"Oh, Laurel, we got some good news today."

My heart sped. "Tell me."

"The tumors are shrinking. The chemotherapy is working, Laurel. It's working."

I gripped the phone and nodded, as though Mom could see me. "That's wonderful."

"It's too early to be sure, Laurel. But it's the most we could hope for. And it's happening."

"I'm glad."

"So, Laurel, how's everything on your end?"

"Fine, Mom."

"Really?"

It wasn't really. But Mom was almost happy now. I wasn't about to spoil it for her.

"Really, Mom."

"Laurel, have I told you how proud I am of you?"

I laughed. "What do you mean, Mom?"

"I'm so proud of you for the way you're handling this rabbit thing."

I swallowed hard. "I'm not handling it very well, Mom. The survival rate isn't great."

"Oh, Laurel. Don't you see? Have you ever heard of the syndrome called failure to thrive?"

"No."

"It happens sometimes with babies. Human babies. They can be born perfectly healthy, but something goes wrong; they think something goes wrong between the mother and the baby, and the babies just stop eating. And they can die."

"How awful."

"But with your rabbits, Laurel, it's been just the opposite. They were born with almost no chance at all. But you poured all your love into them, and you've done something no one thought you could do. They've been dying, yes. But no one expected them to live past a few days."

"That doesn't seem like much, Mom."

"You gave them a chance. And if any of them make it, it will be because of how strong your love is."

"I don't know if any of them will make it, Mom."

"I know you don't. You're brave, Laurel. You go on trying in the face of death. It's the bravest thing anyone can do. You've been a great help to me these past few weeks. Just watching you has helped me so much."

"I love you, Mom."

"Good night, Laurel. I love you, too."

11

Alive

We buried Binky on Tuesday morning before we went to school. I hated to leave Blossom alone all day. She wasn't actually alone, since Bun Bun was there. But Bun Bun showed her no love. Blossom would have no one to cuddle with, no one to lick or be licked by.

During recess, I told Charlotte.

"That's sad," she said. "They'll all be dead soon, and I'll never have gotten to see a single one of them."

Suddenly I blurted out, "Come home with me today."

Charlotte's eyes went wide. "Do you mean it? I thought you were worried about germs."

"I mean it. You have to see Blossom. You have to hold her and feel how soft her fur is and watch her fall over when she hops."

"I'll wash my hands five times. Six. And I'll tie a handkerchief around my nose so I don't breathe on her. And . . ."

"It's okay, Charlotte. We'll both wash our hands. But if she dies, Charlotte, it won't be your fault."

"That's right. It's Bun Bun's fault."

"No, it's not!"

"Of course it is," said Charlotte.

"Bun Bun doesn't understand anything," I said. "She doesn't even seem to know Blossom's her baby."

"Well, then, you see? She screwed up."

"No." I thought of Bun Bun sniffing at the babies. I thought of her hiding from them in the corner of the cage. "Something screwed up, but it probably wasn't Bun Bun. She was a baby when I got her. Who knows when the breeders took her away from her mother and sold her to the pet store? She probably doesn't know the first thing about rabbit culture." I sat down on a frozen bench by the monkey bars. "We can't blame Bun Bun. We can't blame anyone."

Charlotte sighed and sank down beside me. "Motherless bunnies."

"Blossom's got me," I said.

"And how much do you know about bunny culture?" Charlotte laced her gloved fingers together and dropped them in her lap.

I couldn't get her question out of my head for the rest of the day.

When we got home, Arthur led the way down the basement stairs, and I let him have the honor of putting Blossom in Charlotte's hands. Blossom was going wild with hunger. She nuzzled at Charlotte's palm. I warmed up the formula and handed the bottle to Charlotte.

Charlotte looked at me in amazement. "I can feed her? Oh, thank you, Laurel. Thank you, thank you." She tipped the bottle delicately toward Blossom. A week ago, such a slight movement wouldn't have worked at all. But today it worked just fine. Blossom knew the routine well. She opened her mouth and latched on to the bottle and guzzled away. "Oh, she's eating, she's eating. Isn't she darling?"

I smiled proudly.

Arthur beamed with fatherly love. "Yum yum yum," he sang. "Yum yum yum."

Blossom opened her right eye for the very first time. Her eye was shiny black and full of intelligence.

Arthur and I hugged each other in our delight. It was as though a secret had been revealed to us.

Charlotte laughed. "What a smart little thing you are, Blossom Bunny." She touched Blossom's tail, which was now covered with fur and seemed like a proper rabbit tail rather than the cut-off rat tail it used to look like. Blossom peed in Charlotte's hand.

"Like mother, like daughter," I said.

That was six weeks ago. Blossom is an adolescent rabbit now. It turns out he's a *he*, not a *she*, and at first I thought of changing his name to Baxter. But on second thought, I kept him Blossom, because he knows his name (he even comes when called) and I remembered the clerk in Mr. Caldwell's pet store warning me not to give rabbits an identity crisis. Blossom has long ears. One of them flops down—like the lop his father is—and one of them sticks straight back—like the regular rabbit his mother is. No one looks at him without smiling. He's brown and gray and has the softest fur you can imagine. He and Bun Bun have made friends. They huddle together in the cage, which is now outside again, and they seem to groom each other, sort of like cats. In fact, Blossom stands up against the side of the cage when he sees me coming, and when I open the cage, he actually licks my hand affectionately. I usually take him out and bring him into the kitchen. I lay him down on his back in my lap, and I pet his tummy. He loves that. Half the time he falls asleep with his little paws in the air. I drew a picture of him sleeping.

Now and then, Arthur scoops Blossom off my lap and rolls him up into what he calls a bunny ball. He holds Blossom to his ear and swears he can hear a purr. That's when we think about that kitty formula. But the formula days are long past; when Blossom was just a little over three weeks old, he started eating Tasteeos. And now he eats whatever I give Bun Bun. He's a pig.

He's also very smart. If I put him on my bedroom floor while I'm hanging from my bar, he hops around me in wonder, but he never goes directly under my feet. I think he might actually know he'd get squashed if I fell on him. I'm still trying to hang a little longer every day, though I've cut back to just one hanging a day now, not the three I did when I used to feed Blossom with a bottle. My back will take patience (Mom says), because people change a lot more slowly than baby rabbits.

Like Arthur. He still has a habit of saying crazy things. Take the other day. We were sitting in the kitchen and watching Blossom hop around the floor, stopping every few seconds to rub his chin on the edge of the onion bin or on a chair leg or even on Arthur's and my shoes.

"He's always got an itch," said Arthur.

"He's got scent glands under his chin. When he rubs like that, he leaves his smell. That's his way of saying, 'This belongs to me.' "

"Ha!" Arthur jumped up. "I belong to Blossom. So do you, Laurel. Ha ha ha." Arthur did a little dance around the table. "So Blossom has scent glands, and Bun Bun has memory glands."

"Memory glands?"

"Yeah. On her tummy. Only she doesn't remember too good, I don't think."

"*Mammary glands*, Arthur. They have nothing to do with memory. They're where an animal makes milk for its babies."

Arthur frowned. I felt sorry for him. The world

seemed to be full of words that stumped Arthur. But just when I was about to say something comforting, he hopped off into the dining room, stopping every few seconds to rub his chin against a piece of furniture and say, "Mine mine mine."

The big problem, of course, is that Blossom can't stay with Bun Bun once he's six months old, because he'll try to mate with her, and they'll probably have babies that are deformed or demented or both. I thought of getting a second cage, but somehow having two rabbits and never letting them be together seems like torture. I couldn't bear that. But I found a solution I think I can bear. It will hurt, but any solution would. Charlotte desperately loves Blossom, and he's the first animal she's ever loved. She's been talking about buying a gray hair spray so she can spot her hair to match Blossom's fur. It didn't even occur to her to dye Blossom's fur to match her hair. She finally understands. So I spoke to her mother privately. On May 8, Charlotte's birthday, I'm giving her Blossom.

Mom's much happier these days. Aunt Lizzy's tumors have shrunk, and after Easter, her six months of chemotherapy will be over. Then we'll see what happens. As Mom says, there's no guarantee; we can only hope. But that's the way life is. None of us have a guarantee. We hope.

And now and then, there's a Blossom to keep us hoping.

And, oh yes, Dr. Steinway and I have talked a lot on the phone lately. He was amazed when I told him about Blossom surviving. He said I had a golden touch. We got to talking, and I told him about the other animals I've had over the years. He asked me how I'd taken care of all of them. Then he asked how I had cared for Bun Bun's litter. He took my name and phone number. Then, out of the blue, he called me about a new patient of his who owns a rabbit, and the rabbit keeps having problems. It has this thing about corn, and it got into the cereal cupboard and ate a whole box of cornflakes and couldn't move for a day. So Dr. Steinway called me to talk about this rabbit. And we decided together what to advise the owner. (The advice was simple—lock the cereal cupboard and watch the rabbit better.) Anyway, Dr. Steinway asked me to work for him this summer. Just part-time. And he'll pay me ten dollars a week. But I'd have done it for nothing. I asked Mom first, because it's a long way to ride my bike and Mom gets nervous about those things. But when she understood how important it was to me, she said okay, and I said to him, "You bet." I've begun my preparation. I'm trying to read all the books on animal care at our town's public library. I don't want to disappoint Dr. Steinway. There's a lot of work to do.